RAINBOW magic®

My RAINBOW FAIRIES Collection

Special thanks to
Narinder Dhami and
Sue Bentley

ORCHARD BOOKS
Carmelite House
50 Victoria Embankment
London EC4Y 0DZ

Original edition of *Flora the Fancy Dress Fairy* published
by Orchard Books in 2007
Original edition of *The Rainbow Magic Treasury* published
by Orchard Books in 2007

A CIP catalogue record for this book is available
from the British Library.

ISBN 978 1 40832 974 0

5 7 9 10 8 6 4
Printed in China
Orchard Books is a division of Hachette Children's Books,
an Hachette UK company.
www.hachette.co.uk

RAINBOW magic®

My RAINBOW FAIRIES Collection

Daisy Meadows

ORCHARD

Hello, Fairy Friend!

Welcome to the Rainbow
Fairies Collection!

Inside this book are all our
original stories and a special edition
of Flora the Fancy Dress Fairy.
You'll also meet Jack Frost
and his naughty goblins!

So let the magic come to you and
discover the wonderful world
of Rainbow Magic!

All our love,

Saffron
x

Fern
x

Flora
x

Ruby
x

Amber
x

Sky
x

Izzy
x

Heather
x

A Sprinkling Of Rainbow Magic

Read all about Ruby the Red Fairy.
Here she is with her six rainbow sisters!

The seven
Rainbow Fairies
have each cast a special
friendship spell for you.
Try reading them out
to your best friend!

Ruby the Red Fairy

My spell is for smiles and
a thousand kind acts.
Making a friend
is a wonderful pact!

Amber the Orange Fairy

My spell is for parties and
meeting to play!
Chatting with friends will
brighten your day.

Saffron the Yellow Fairy

My spell is for being
there no matter what.
A friend you can count
on is worth such a lot!

Good times and bad...

When Jack Frost didn't get invited to the Midsummer Ball, he caused so much trouble! The ice lord took the colours away from Fairyland by banishing the Rainbow Fairies to the human world. Thank goodness Kirsty and Rachel were there to help them – true friends in times of need!

Heather the Violet Fairy

My spell is for help,
splitting problems in two.
You'll never know when you
friend may need you!

Izzy the Indigo Fairy

My spell is for giggle,
for laughs in the sun.
Friendship is priceless,
but most of all fun!

Sky the Blue Fairy

My spell is for whispers
and secrets to share.
Open your heart to
someone who'll care!

Fern the Green Fairy

My spell is for trying
out daring new things.
Do them together,
you'll be lifted on wings!

Meet Jack Frost and the Goblins

Jack Frost has an army of naughty goblins to help him create chaos. Whenever there's a chill in the air, the fairies must be on their guard...

I will have my revenge for not being invited to the Fairyland Midsummer Ball!

Name
Jack Frost.

Favourite colour
Ice-white.

Personality
Cold-hearted, jealous and mean.

Home
His turreted frozen Ice Castle.

Frosty friends
Only his band of grumpy goblin servants.

Most trusted magic
His powerful banishment spell.

Frosty features
A chill breeze always swirls around Jack's bony figure and angry face. His ice-blue robes are trimmed with sharp icicles. Frost glints in his white hair and beard. His pointy elf boots leave icy footprints behind him.

Horrible hobby
Jack thinks he's a magnificent artist. He's always etching frozen designs on window panes, but the act that no one ever seems to notice them never fails to put him in a frosty mood.

Name
The Goblins.

Personality
Selfish, sneaky but very dim.

Home
The dungeons of Jack Frost's Ice Castle.

Favourite food
Goblins are so greedy they'll eat anything, even dog food!

Horrible hobby
Taking fairy possessions and trampling on flowers.

> ❋ We're always ready to cause mischief! ❋

Frosty friends
None. Most goblins even fight amongst themselves.

Worst time of year
Unfortunately it's winter. Jack Frost gives them lots of jobs to do and goblins hate having cold feet!

Frosty features
The tallest goblins are as high as Kirsty and Rachel's waists, but Jack Frost often uses his powers to make them taller or smaller! All goblins are ugly green creatures with big feet and sharp, pointy ears and noses.

Cold winds blow and thick ice form,
I conjure up this fairy storm.
To seven corners of the mortal world
the Rainbow Fairies will be hurled!

I curse every part of Fairyland,
with a frosty wave of my icy hand.
For now and always, from this fateful day,
Fairyland will be cold and grey!

Contents

Ruby
the Red
Fairy

Ruby the
Red Fairy

"Look, Dad!" said Rachel Walker. She pointed across the blue-green sea at the rocky island ahead of them.

"Is that Rainspell Island?" she asked.

Her dad nodded. "Yes. Our holiday is about to begin!"

The waves slapped against the side of the ferry and Rachel felt her heart thump with excitement.

Suddenly, a few fat raindrops plopped down onto her head. "Oh!" she gasped.

Rachel's mum grabbed her hand.

"Let's go inside," she said.

"Isn't that strange?" Rachel said.

"The sun is still shining!"

"Let's hope the rain stops before we arrive," said
Mr Walker.

Rachel looked out of the window. A girl was
standing alone on the deck, staring up at the sky.
Rachel slipped back outside to see what was so
interesting.

High above them was the most amazing rainbow
that Rachel had ever seen.

One end of the rainbow was far out to sea. The other seemed to fall somewhere on Rainspell Island.

"Isn't it perfect?" the dark-haired girl whispered to Rachel.

"Yes, it is," Rachel agreed. "Are you going to Rainspell on holiday?"

The girl nodded. "I'm Kirsty Tate," she said.

Rachel smiled. "I'm Rachel Walker. We're staying at Mermaid Cottage," she added.

"And we're at Dolphin Cottage," said Kirsty. "Do you think we might be near each other?"

"I hope so," Rachel replied. She had a feeling she was going to like Kirsty.

The ferry sailed into Rainspell's tiny harbour. Seagulls flew around them, and fishing boats bobbed on the water.

"There you are, Rachel!" called Mrs Walker.

Rachel saw her mum and dad coming on to the deck.

"Mum, Dad, this is Kirsty," said Rachel. "She's staying at Dolphin Cottage."

"That's right next door to ours," said Mr Walker. "I remember seeing it on the map."

Rachel and Kirsty looked at each other in delight.

"I'd better go and find my mum and dad," said Kirsty. She looked round. "Oh, here they are."

Kirsty's mum and dad came over to say hello. Then the ferry docked, and everyone began to leave the boat.

Mermaid Cottage and Dolphin Cottage were right next to the beach. Rachel loved her bedroom in the attic. From the window, she could see
the waves rolling onto
the sand. A shout from
outside made her
look down.

Kirsty was standing under the window, waving
at her.

"Let's go and explore the beach!" she called. Rachel
dashed outside. Seaweed lay in piles on the sand, and
there were tiny pink and white shells dotted about.

"I love it here already!" Rachel shouted happily
above the noise of the seagulls.

"Me too," Kirsty said. She pointed up at the sky.
"Look, the rainbow's still there."

Sure enough, the rainbow glowed brightly among
the fluffy white clouds.

"Have you heard the story about the pot of gold at
the end of the rainbow?" Kirsty asked.

Rachel nodded. "Yes, but that's just in fairy stories,"
she said.

Kirsty grinned. "Maybe. Let's go and find out for
ourselves!"

"OK," Rachel agreed.

They rushed back to tell their parents they were going for a walk. Then they set off along the lane. It led away from the beach, towards a small wood.

Rachel kept looking up at the rainbow. She was worried that it would start to fade now that the rain had stopped. But the colours stayed clear and bright.

"It looks like the end of the rainbow is over there," Kirsty said. "Come on!" And she hurried towards the trees.

The wood was cool and green after the heat of the sun. Rachel and Kirsty followed a winding path until they came to a clearing. Then they both stopped and stared.

The rainbow shone down onto the grass through a gap in the trees.

And there, at the rainbow's end, lay an old, black pot.

"There really is a pot of gold!" Kirsty exclaimed.

"It could just be a cooking pot," Rachel said. "Some campers might have left it behind."

But Kirsty shook her head. "I don't think so," she said. "It looks really old."

The pot was sitting on the grass, upside down.

"Let's have a closer look," said Kirsty. She tried to turn it over. "It's heavy!" she gasped. Rachel went to help her. They pushed and pushed at the pot. This time it moved, just a little.

"Let's try again," Kirsty panted.

"Are you ready, Rachel?"

Tap! Tap! Tap!

"What was that?" Rachel gasped

"I don't know," whispered Kirsty.

Tap! Tap!

Kirsty looked down. "I think it's coming from inside the pot!"

Rachel's eyes opened wide. "Are you sure?" She bent down, and put her ear to the pot. *Tap! Tap!* Then, to her amazement, Rachel heard a tiny voice.

"Help!" it called. "Help me!"

Rachel grabbed Kirsty's arm. "Did you hear that?"

Kirsty nodded. "Quick!" she said. "We must turn the pot over!"

Rachel and Kirsty pushed at the pot as hard as they could.

It began to rock from side to side.

"We're nearly there!" Rachel panted.

Suddenly, the pot rolled on to its side. A shower of sparkling red dust flew out of it. And there, right in the middle of the glittering cloud, was a tiny girl with wings!

Rachel and Kirsty watched in
wonder as the tiny girl fluttered in the
sunlight, her delicate wings sparkling
with all the colours of the rainbow.

"Oh, Rachel!" Kirsty whispered.
"It's a fairy…"

The fairy fluttered
just above Rachel
and Kirsty. Her
short, silky dress
was the colour of
strawberries. Red earrings glowed in her ears. Her
golden hair was plaited with tiny red roses, and she
wore crimson slippers on her little feet.

She waved her wand and a shower of sparkling red
fairy dust floated softly down to the ground. Where it
landed, all sorts of red flowers appeared with a pop!

Rachel and Kirsty watched open-mouthed. It really and truly was a fairy.

"This is like a dream," Rachel said.

"I always believed in fairies," said Kirsty. "But I never thought I'd see one!"

The fairy flew towards them. "Oh, thank you so much!" she called in a tiny, silvery voice. "I'm free at last!" She glided down, and landed on Kirsty's hand.

Kirsty gasped. The fairy felt lighter and softer than a butterfly.

"I was beginning to think I'd never get out of that pot!" said the fairy. "Tell me your names, quickly. There's so much to be done, and we must get started right away."

Rachel wondered what the fairy meant. "I'm Rachel," she said.

"And I'm Kirsty," said Kirsty.

"I'm the Red Rainbow Fairy – but you can call me Ruby," the fairy replied.

"Ruby..." Kirsty breathed. "A Rainbow Fairy..."

"Yes," said Ruby. "I have six sisters: Amber, Saffron, Fern, Sky, Izzy and Heather. One for each colour of the rainbow, you see. It's our job to put all the different colours into Fairyland," she explained.

"Why were you shut up inside that old pot?" said Rachel.

"And where are your sisters?" Kirsty added.

Ruby's wings drooped and her eyes filled with tears. "I don't know," she said. "Something terrible has happened in Fairyland. We need your help!"

"Of course we'll help you!"
Kirsty said.

Ruby wiped her eyes.

"Thank you!"

she said. "First I must

show you something. Follow me – as quickly as you

can!" She flew into the air, her wings shimmering in

the sunshine.

Rachel and Kirsty followed Ruby across the clearing.

The fairy stopped by a pond under a willow tree.

"Look!" she said. "I can show you what happened

yesterday."

She flew over the pond and scattered another shower

of sparkling fairy dust with her wand. The water lit up

with a strange, silver light.

Rachel and Kirsty watched in astonishment as a

picture appeared. It was like looking through a window

into another land!

A river of brightest blue ran past hills of greenest green. Scattered on the hillsides were red and white toadstool houses. And on top of the highest hill stood a silver palace with four pink towers.

The towers were so high, their points were almost hidden by the fluffy white clouds.

Hundreds of fairies were making their way towards the palace. Rachel and Kirsty could see elves, pixies and sprites too. Everyone seemed very excited.

"Yesterday was the day of the Fairyland Midsummer Ball," Ruby explained. She pointed with her wand. "There I am, with my Rainbow sisters."

Kirsty and Rachel saw seven fairies, each dressed prettily in their own rainbow colour.

"The Midsummer Ball is very special," Ruby went on. "My sisters and I are in charge of sending out invitations."

To the sound of tinkling music, the front doors of the palace slowly opened.

"Here come King Oberon and Queen Titania," said Ruby. "The Fairy King and Queen."

Kirsty and Rachel watched as the King and Queen stepped out. The King wore a splendid golden coat and golden crown.

His queen wore a silver dress and a tiara that sparkled with diamonds. Everyone cheered. After a while, the King signalled for quiet. "Fairies, elves, pixies and sprites," he began. "Welcome to the Midsummer Ball!"

The fairies clapped and cheered again.

Suddenly, a grey mist filled the picture. Kirsty and Rachel watched in alarm as all the fairies started to shiver. A loud, chilly voice shouted out, "Stop the music!"

A tall, bony figure was pushing his way through the crowd. He was dressed all in white, and there was

frost on his white hair and beard. Icicles hung from his clothes. But his face was red and angry. Everyone looked scared.

"Who's that?" Rachel asked with a shiver.

"Jack Frost," said Ruby.

Jack Frost glared at the seven Rainbow Fairies.

"Why wasn't I invited to the Midsummer Ball?"
he asked coldly.

The Rainbow Fairies gasped in horror...

Ruby looked up from the pond picture. "Yes, we forgot
to invite Jack Frost," she said.

In the pond picture, the Fairy Queen stepped forward.

"You are very welcome, Jack Frost," she said. "Please
stay and enjoy the ball."

But Jack Frost just looked angrier. "Too late!" he
hissed. "You forgot to invite me!" He pointed a thin,
icy finger at the Rainbow Fairies.

"You will not forget this!" he snarled. "My spell will
banish the Rainbow Fairies to the seven corners of
the mortal world. From this day on, Fairyland will be
without colour – for ever!"

An icy wind began to blow. It picked up the seven
Rainbow Fairies and spun them up into the sky.
The other fairies watched in dismay.

Jack Frost turned to the King and Queen. "Your
Rainbow Fairies will never return!" he cackled. He
walked away, leaving a trail of icy footprints.

The Fairy Queen lifted her silver wand. "I cannot
undo Jack Frost's magic completely," she cried. "But
I can guide the Rainbow Fairies to a safe place where
they will be rescued!"

She pointed her wand at the sky. A black pot came spinning through the stormy clouds. One by one, the Rainbow Fairies tumbled into the pot.

"Pot-at-the-end-of-the-rainbow, keep our Rainbow Fairies safely together," the Queen called. "And take them to Rainspell Island!"

The pot flew out of sight, behind a dark cloud. At once the bright colours of Fairyland began to fade, until it looked like an old black and white photograph.

"Oh no!" Kirsty gasped. The picture in the pond vanished.

"The Fairy Queen cast her own spell!" Rachel said. "She put you and your sisters in the pot, and sent you to Rainspell."

Ruby nodded. "Rainspell is a place full of magic. She knew we'd be safe here."

"But where are your sisters?" asked Kirsty. "They were in the pot too."

Ruby looked upset. "Jack Frost's spell was very strong," she said.

"As the pot spun through the sky, the wind blew my sisters out again. I was at the bottom, so I was safe. But I was trapped when the pot landed upside down."

"So your sisters are somewhere on Rainspell?" Kirsty said.

Ruby nodded. "They're scattered all over the island. Jack Frost's spell has trapped them too." She flew onto Kirsty's shoulder. "That's where you and Rachel come in."

"How?" Rachel asked.

"You found me, didn't you?" the fairy said. "So you could rescue my Rainbow sisters too! Then we can all bring colour back to Fairyland."

"Of course we'll search for your sisters," Kirsty said.

"Won't we, Rachel?" Rachel nodded.

"Oh, thank you," Ruby said happily.

"But we're only here for a week," Rachel said.

"We must get started right away," said Ruby. "First, I must take you to Fairyland to meet the King and Queen."

"You're taking us to Fairyland?" Kirsty gasped.

"But how will we get there?" Rachel said.

"We'll fly there," Ruby replied.

"But we can't fly!" Rachel pointed out.

Ruby smiled. She whirled up into the air and swirled her wand above them. Magic red fairy dust fluttered down.

Rachel and Kirsty began to feel a bit strange. Were the trees getting bigger or were they getting smaller?

They were getting smaller!

Smaller and smaller and smaller, until they were the same size as Ruby.

"I'm tiny!" Rachel laughed. She was so small, the flowers around her seemed like trees.

Kirsty twisted round to look at her back. She had shiny, delicate wings!

Ruby beamed. "Let's go!"

Rachel twitched her shoulders. Her wings fluttered, and she felt herself rise up into the air. She was quite wobbly at first!

"Help!" Kirsty yelled, as she shot up into the air. "I'm not very good at this!"

"Come on," said Ruby, taking their hands. "I'll help you." She led them up, out of the glade.

Rachel looked down on Rainspell Island. She could see the cottages next to the beach, and the harbour.

"Where is Fairyland, Ruby?" Kirsty asked.

"It's so far away, that no mortal could ever find it," Ruby said.

They flew through the clouds for a long, long time. At last Ruby turned to them and smiled. "We're here," she said.

As they flew down, Kirsty and Rachel saw places they recognised from the pond picture: the palace, the hillsides, the toadstool houses. But there were no bright colours now. Because of Jack Frost's spell, everything was a drab shade of grey. Even the air felt cold and damp.

A few fairies walked miserably across the hillsides. Their wings hung limply down their backs.

Suddenly one of the fairies looked up. "Look!" she shouted. "It's Ruby!"

At once, the fairies flew up to meet Ruby, Kirsty and Rachel.

"Have you come from Rainspell, Ruby?"

"Where are the other Rainbow Fairies?"

"Who are your friends?" said another fairy.

"First, we must see the King and Queen," said Ruby. "Then I will tell you everything!"

King Oberon and Queen Titania were seated on their thrones. Their palace was as grey as everywhere else in Fairyland. But they smiled warmly when Ruby arrived with Rachel and Kirsty.

"Welcome back, Ruby," said the Queen. "We have missed you."

"Your Majesties, these are my friends, Kirsty and Rachel. They believe in magic!" Ruby announced. She told everyone how Rachel and Kirsty had rescued her.

"Will you help us to find Ruby's Rainbow sisters?" the Queen asked.

"Yes, we will," Kirsty said.

"How will we know where to look?" said Rachel, feeling worried.

"Don't worry," said the Queen. "The magic you need to find each Rainbow Fairy will find you. Just wait and see."

King Oberon rubbed his beard. "You have six days of your holiday left, and six fairies to find," he said. "That's a lot of fairy-finding. You will need some special help." He nodded at one of his footmen, a plump frog in a buttoned-up jacket.

The frog hopped over to Rachel and Kirsty and handed them each a tiny, silver bag.

"The bags contain magic tools," the Queen told them. "Open them only when you really need  to, and you will find something to help you."

"Look!" shouted another frog footman. "Ruby is beginning to fade!"

Rachel and Kirsty looked at Ruby in horror.

The fairy was growing paler! Her lovely dress was no longer red but pink, and her golden hair was turning white.

"Jack Frost's magic is still at work," said the King. "We cannot undo his spell until all the Rainbow Fairies are together again."

"Quick, Ruby!" urged the Queen. "You must return to Rainspell at once."

Ruby, Kirsty and Rachel flew into the air.

"Don't worry!" Kirsty called. "We'll be back with all the Rainbow Fairies very soon!"

"Good luck!" called the King and Queen.

As they flew further away from Fairyland, Ruby's colour began to return. Soon she was bright and sparkling again.

When they reached Rainspell again, they landed in
the clearing next to the old, black pot. Ruby scattered
fairy dust over Rachel and Kirsty. There was a puff of
glittering red smoke,
and the two girls shot up to their normal size. Rachel

wriggled her shoulders. Her
wings had gone.

"I loved being a fairy,"
Kirsty said.

They watched as Ruby
sprinkled her magic dust
over the old, black pot.

"What are you doing?"
Rachel asked.

"Jack Frost's magic means
that I can't help you look for
my sisters," Ruby explained. "I will wait for you here,
in the pot-at-the-end-of-the-rainbow."

Suddenly the pot began to move. It rolled across the grass, and stopped under the weeping willow tree.

"The pot will be hidden under the tree," said Ruby. "I'll be safe there."

"We'd better start looking for the other Rainbow

Fairies," Rachel said to Kirsty. "Where shall we start?"

Ruby shook her head. "Remember what the Queen said," she told them. "The magic will come to you."

She flew into the air. "Goodbye, and good luck!"

"We'll be back soon, Ruby," said Kirsty.

"And we're going to find *all* your Rainbow sisters," Rachel promised.

Amber
the Orange Fairy

Amber the Orange Fairy

"What a lovely day!" Rachel Walker cried. She and her friend, Kirsty Tate, were running along Rainspell Island's yellow, sandy beach. Their parents walked a little way behind them.

"It's a magical day," Kirsty added with a grin.

As they ran, they passed rock pools that shone like jewels in the sunshine.

Rachel spotted a little *splash!* in one of the pools.

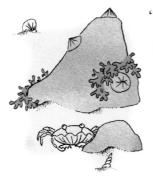

"There's something in there, Kirsty!" She pointed. "Let's go and look."

Kirsty's heart thumped as she gazed into the crystal clear water. Suddenly, the water rippled.

A little brown crab scuttled across the sandy bottom and vanished under a rock. Kirsty felt disappointed. "I thought it might be another Rainbow Fairy," she said.

Rachel sighed. "Never mind. We'll have to keep looking."

"Of course we will," Kirsty agreed.

Rachel looked at the shimmering blue sea. "Shall we have a swim?"

But Kirsty wasn't listening. "Look over there, by those rocks," she said.

Rachel saw something sparkling in the sunshine. She hurried over and picked up a piece of shiny purple foil.

"It's just the wrapper from a chocolate bar," she said sadly.

"Do you remember what the Fairy Queen said?"
Kirsty asked.

Rachel nodded. "Let the magic come to you," she
said. "You're right, Kirsty. We should wait for the magic
to happen. After all, that's how we found Ruby, isn't
it?" She put her beach bag on the sand. "Come on –
race you into the sea!"

They rushed into the water and splashed about until
they got goosebumps.

Then they walked along the beach looking for
shells. They found long, thin, blue shells and tiny, round,

white shells.
Soon their
hands were
full. They had
walked right
round the curve
of the bay.

Rachel looked over her shoulder.

"Look how far we've come," she said.

Kirsty stopped. A gust of wind tugged at her T-shirt and she shivered. "It's getting cold now," she said. "Shall we go back?"

"Yes, it must be nearly teatime," said Rachel.

They began to walk back along the beach.

"That's funny," said Kirsty. "It's not windy here."

They looked back and saw little swirls of sand being blown around where they'd just been. The two friends looked at each other with excitement.

"It's magic," Kirsty whispered. "It has to be!"

They walked back and the breeze swirled around their legs again. Then the sand began to drift to one side, as if invisible hands were pushing it away.

A large scallop shell appeared, much bigger than the other shells on the beach. It was pearly white with soft orange streaks, and it was tightly closed.

The girls knelt down on the sand, spilling the little shells out of their hands. Kirsty was about to pick up the scallop shell when Rachel put out her hand.

"Listen," she whispered.

Inside the shell, a tiny, silvery voice was humming... Very carefully, Rachel picked up the shell.

The humming stopped at once.

"I mustn't be scared," said the tiny voice. "I just have to be brave, and help will come very soon."

"Hello," Kirsty whispered.

"Is there a fairy in there?"

"Yes!" cried the voice. "I'm Amber the Orange Fairy! Can you get me out of here?"

"Of course we will," Kirsty promised. "My name is Kirsty, and my friend Rachel is here too." She looked up at Rachel. "We've found another Rainbow Fairy!"

"Quick," Rachel said. "Let's get the shell open." She took hold of the scallop shell and tried to pull the two halves apart. Nothing happened.

"Try again," said Kirsty. She and Rachel each grasped one half of the shell and tugged. But the shell stayed tightly shut.

"What's happening?" Amber called.

51

"We can't open the shell," Kirsty said. "But we'll think of something." She turned to Rachel. "If we find a piece of driftwood, we could use it to open the shell."

Rachel glanced around. "I can't see any driftwood," she said. "We could try tapping the shell on a rock."

"But that might hurt Amber," Kirsty said.

Suddenly Rachel remembered something. "What about the magic bags the Fairy Queen gave us?"

"Of course!" Kirsty put her face close to the shell

again. "Amber, we're going to look in our magic bags."

"OK, but please hurry," Amber called.

Rachel opened her beach bag. The two magic bags were hidden under her towel. One of the bags was glowing with a golden light.

"Open it, quick," Kirsty whispered.

As Rachel undid the bag, a fountain of glittering
sparks flew out.

She slid her hand into the bag. She could feel
something light and soft inside.
She pulled it out, scattering
sparkles everywhere. It was
a shimmering golden
feather.

Rachel tried to use the
feather to push the two
halves of the shell apart.
But the feather just curled
up in her hand.

"Maybe we should ask Amber how to open the shell
with the feather," said Rachel.

"Amber, we've looked in the magic bags," Kirsty said,
"and we've found a feather."

"Oh, good!" Amber said happily.

"But we don't know what to do with it," Rachel added.

Amber laughed. It sounded like the tinkle of a tiny bell. "You tickle the shell, of course!"

"Let's give it a try," Kirsty said.

Rachel began to tickle the shell with the feather. At first nothing happened. Then they heard a soft, gritty chuckle. Then another and another. Slowly the two halves of the shell began to open.

"It's working," Kirsty gasped. "Keep tickling, Rachel!"

The shell was laughing hard now. The two halves opened wider…

And there, sitting inside the smooth, peach-coloured shell, was Amber the Orange Fairy.

"I'm free!" Amber cried joyfully.

She shot out of the shell and up into the air. Orange fairy dust floated down around Kirsty and Rachel. It turned into orange bubbles as it fell. One of the bubbles landed on Rachel's arm and burst with a tiny *POP!*

"The bubbles smell like oranges!" Rachel smiled.

Amber turned cartwheels through the sky. "Thank you!" she called.

She wore a shiny orange catsuit and long boots. Her flame-coloured hair was tied in a ponytail with a band of peach blossoms. She held an orange wand tipped with gold.

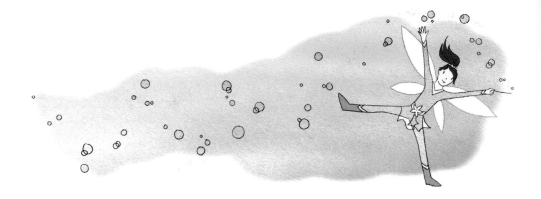

"I'm so glad you found me!" Amber cried.
"But who are you? And where are my Rainbow sisters?"

Suddenly she stopped. She floated down and landed
softly on Rachel's hand. "I'm sorry," she said with a
smile. "I've been shut up in this shell ever since Jack
Frost's spell banished us from Fairyland. How did you
know where to find me?"

"Kirsty and I promised your sister Ruby that we
would look for all the Rainbow Fairies," Rachel told her.

"Ruby?" Amber's face lit up. "You've found Ruby?"

"Yes, she's quite safe," Rachel said. "She's in the pot-at-
the-end-of-the-rainbow under a willow tree."

Amber did a backflip. "Please take me to her!" she begged.

"I'll ask our parents if we can go for a walk," Kirsty said. She ran across the beach and quickly came back. "Mum said that's fine," she panted.

"Let's go!" Amber called. She flew up and did a somersault in mid-air.

Rachel pulled their shorts, T-shirts and trainers out of her beach bag and both girls put them on.

"Rachel, could you bring my shell?" Amber asked.

Rachel looked surprised. "Yes, of course," she said.

"It's really comfy," Amber explained. "It will make a lovely bed for me and my sisters."

Rachel put the shell in her beach bag, and they set off with Amber sitting cross-legged on Kirsty's shoulder.

"My wings are a bit stiff after being in the shell," she said. "I don't think I can fly very far yet."

The girls reached the clearing where the pot-at-the-end-of-the-rainbow was hidden.

The pot was where they'd left it, under the weeping willow tree. But climbing out of it was a big, green frog.

"Oh no!" Rachel cried. Where was Ruby?

Rachel dashed forward and grabbed the frog round his plump, green tummy. The frog glared at her.

"What do you think you're doing?" he croaked.

Rachel was so shocked, she let go of the frog.

He hopped away, looking very annoyed.

"It's a talking frog!" Kirsty gasped.

"Bertram!" Amber flew down from
Kirsty's shoulder and threw her arms
around the frog. "Thank goodness
you're safe, Miss Amber!" said the frog.

Amber beamed at Rachel and Kirsty. "Bertram isn't
an ordinary frog," she explained. "He's one of King
Oberon's footmen."

"Oh, yes!" said Kirsty. "We saw the frog footmen
when we went to the palace in Fairyland with Ruby."

"But they were wearing purple uniforms then,"
Rachel added.

"A frog in a purple uniform
would not be a good idea on
Rainspell Island," Bertram
pointed out. "It's much
better if I look like an
ordinary frog."

"What are you doing here, Bertram?" asked Amber. "Where's Ruby?"

"Don't worry," Bertram replied. "Miss Ruby is safe in the pot." He looked very stern. "King Oberon sent me to Rainspell. The Cloud Fairies spotted Jack Frost's goblins sneaking out of Fairyland. We think he has sent them here to stop the Rainbow Fairies being found."

Kirsty felt a shiver run down her spine.

"Jack Frost's goblins?" she said.

"They're his servants," Amber explained. Her wings trembled and she looked very scared. "They want to keep Fairyland cold and grey!"

"I'll look after you, Miss Amber," Bertram croaked.

Suddenly a shower of red fairy dust shot out of the pot. Ruby fluttered out. "Amber!" she shouted joyfully. "They found you!"

"Ruby!" Amber called. She cartwheeled towards her sister.

The air around them fizzed with tiny red flowers and orange bubbles.

"Thank you, Kirsty and Rachel," said Ruby. She and Amber floated down to them, holding hands. "It's so good to have Amber back safely."

"What about you?" Rachel
asked. "Have you been all right
in the pot?"

Ruby nodded. "I'm fine now
that Bertram is here," she replied.
"I've been making the pot into a
fairy home."

"I've brought my shell with me,"
Amber said. "It will make a lovely bed for us. Show her,
Rachel."

Rachel took the peach-coloured shell out of her bag.

"It's beautiful," said Ruby. She smiled at Rachel
and Kirsty. "Would you like to come and see our new
home?"

"But the pot's too small for Kirsty and me to get
inside," Rachel pointed out. Then she began to tingle
with excitement. "Are you going to make us fairy size
again?"

Ruby nodded. She and Amber flew over the girls'
heads, showering them with fairy dust. Rachel and
Kirsty started to shrink, just as they had done before.
Soon they were tiny, the same size as Ruby and Amber.

"Being a fairy is the best thing
ever," Kirsty said happily. She
twisted round to look at her
silvery wings.

"Yes, it is," Rachel agreed.

Bertram hopped over
to the pot.

"I'll wait outside," he croaked.

Ruby took Rachel's hand, and
Amber took Kirsty's. Then the
fairies led them towards the pot.

Rachel and Kirsty fluttered through
the air, dodging a butterfly that was as big as they were.
Its wings felt like velvet as they brushed gently past it.

"I'm getting better at flying!"
Kirsty laughed as she landed
neatly on the edge of the pot.
She looked down eagerly.

The pot was full of sunlight.
There were little chairs made
from twigs tied with blades of grass. Each chair
had a cushion made from a berry. Rugs of bright green
leaves covered the floor.

"Shall we fetch the shell?" said Rachel.

When they
flew out of the
pot, Bertram
was already
pushing the
shell towards
them across
the grass.

"Here you are,"
he croaked.

The shell seemed very heavy now that Rachel and

Kirsty were the same size as Ruby and Amber. Bertram

helped them to heave it into the pot.

Ruby lined it with sweet-smelling rose petals.

"I wish I could live here too!" said Kirsty.

Ruby turned to her sister. "Do you like it, Amber?"

she asked.

"It's beautiful," Amber replied. "It reminds me of our

house back in Fairyland. I miss it so much."

"Well, I can show you Fairyland,"

Ruby said, "even though we can't go back there yet.

Follow me."

Bertram was still on guard next to the pot when they

flew out again. "Where are you going?" he croaked.

"To the magic pond," Ruby replied. "Come with us."

She sprinkled her magic dust over Rachel and Kirsty.

Quickly, they grew back to
their normal size.

They went over to the pond.
Ruby flew above the water,
scattering fairy dust. Just like
before, a picture began to
appear.

"Fairyland!" Amber
cried, gazing into the water.

Fairyland still looked sad and chilly. The palace, the
toadstool houses, the flowers and the trees were all drab

and grey. Suddenly a
cold breeze rippled the
surface of the water,
and the picture began
to fade.

"What's happening?"
Kirsty whispered.

Another picture was taking shape in the pond – a
thin, grinning face with icicles hanging from his beard.

"It's Jack Frost!" Ruby gasped. As she spoke, the
air turned icy cold and the edges of the pool began
to freeze.

"What's happening?" Rachel asked, shivering.

"This is bad news," said Bertram. "It means that Jack
Frost's goblins are close by!"

The whole pond froze over. Jack Frost's grinning face faded away.

"Follow me," Bertram ordered. He hopped over to a large bush. "We'll hide here."

"Maybe we should go back to the pot," said Ruby.

"Not if the goblins are close by," said Bertram. "We mustn't let them know where the pot is."

The two girls crouched down behind the bush next to Bertram. Ruby and Amber huddled together on Kirsty's shoulder. It was getting colder and colder. Rachel and Kirsty couldn't stop their teeth chattering.

"What are the goblins like?" Rachel whispered.

"They're bigger than us," said Amber, trembling.

"And they have ugly faces and hooked noses and big feet," Ruby added.

"Hush, Miss Ruby," Bertram croaked. "I can hear something."

Rachel saw a hook-nosed shadow flit across the clearing towards them. She grabbed Kirsty's arm. Suddenly the leaves rustled right next to them. They almost jumped out of their skins.

"Oi!" said a gruff voice, sounding very close. "What do you think you're doing?"

Rachel and Kirsty held their breath.

"Nothing," said another gruff voice.

"Goblins!" Amber whispered in Kirsty's ear.

"You stood on my toe," said the first goblin.

"No, I didn't," snapped the other goblin.

"Yes, you did! Keep your big feet to yourself!"

"Well, at least my nose isn't as big as yours!"

The bush shook even more. It sounded as if the goblins were pushing and shoving each other.

"Get out of my way!" one of them shouted. "Ow!"

Rachel and Kirsty looked at each other in alarm. What if the goblins found them there?

"Come on," said one of the goblins. "Jack Frost will be cross if we don't find these fairies. You know he wants us to stop them getting back to Fairyland."

"Well, they're not here, are they?" grumbled the other. "Let's try somewhere else."

The voices died away. The leaves stopped rustling.

Suddenly the air felt warm again. There was a cracking sound as the frozen pond began to melt.

"They've gone," Bertram croaked. "Quick, we must get back to the pot."

They hurried across the clearing. The pot stood under the weeping willow tree, just as before.

"Oh no! Look!" Kirsty cried. "The pot's frozen over!"

The top of the pot was covered with a thick sheet of ice. No one, not even a fairy, could get inside.

"Oh no!" Ruby gasped. "The goblins must have passed really close by!"

She flew over to the pot with Amber right behind her. They drummed on the ice with their tiny fists. But it was too thick for them to break through.

"Shall we try, Rachel?" asked Kirsty. "We could smash the ice with a stick."

But Bertram had another idea. "Stand back, please, everyone," he said.

Suddenly, he leaped forward with a mighty hop. He jumped straight at the sheet of ice, kicking out with his webbed feet. But the ice did not break.

"Try again," he panted.

He jumped forward again and hit the ice. This time, there was a loud cracking sound. One more jump, and the ice shattered into little pieces. Some of it fell inside the pot. Rachel and Kirsty rushed over to fish

72

them out before they melted.

"There you are," Bertram croaked.

"Thank you, Bertram," Ruby called.

She and Amber flew down and hugged the frog.

Bertram looked pleased.

"Just doing my job, Miss Ruby," he said. "You and Miss Amber must stay very close to the pot from now on. It's dangerous for you to go too far."

"We've got to say goodbye to our friends first," Amber told him. She flew into the air, smiling at Rachel and Kirsty.

"Thank you a thousand times."

"We'll see you again soon," said Rachel.

"When we've found your next Rainbow sister," Kirsty added.

"Good luck!" said Ruby. "We'll be waiting here for you." She took her sister's hand, and they flew over to the pot. The two fairies turned to wave at the girls and disappeared inside.

"Don't worry," Bertram said. "I'll look after them."

"We know you will," Rachel said.

She and Kirsty walked out of the wood. "I'm glad Ruby isn't on her own any more," said Rachel.

"I didn't like those goblins," Kirsty said with a shudder. "I hope they don't come back again."

They made their way back to the beach. Their parents were packing away their towels.

"We were just coming to look for you," said Mr Walker.

"Are we going home now?" Rachel asked.

Mr Walker nodded. "It's turned very chilly," he said.

As he spoke, a cold breeze swirled around Rachel and Kirsty. They shivered and looked up at the sky. The sun had disappeared behind a thick, black cloud.

"Jack Frost's goblins are still here!" Kirsty gasped.

"You're right," Rachel agreed. "Let's hope Bertram can keep Ruby and Amber safe while we look for the other Rainbow Fairies!"

Saffron
the Yellow
Fairy

Saffron the Yellow Fairy

"Over here, Kirsty!" Rachel called.

She and Kirsty were running across one of the
emerald green fields on Rainspell Island. Buttercups and
daisies dotted the grass.

"Don't go too far!" Kirsty's mum called.

Kirsty caught up with her friend. Rachel was
standing on the bank of a rippling stream. "What
have you found, Rachel? Is it another
Rainbow Fairy?"

"I'm not sure,"
said Rachel. "I
thought I heard
something."

Kirsty's face lit up.

"Maybe there's a fairy in the stream?"

Rachel knelt down and put her ear close to the water. Kirsty crouched down too and listened hard.

The sun glittered on the water as it splashed over big, shiny pebbles.

Then they heard a tiny bubbling voice. "Follow me..." it gurgled. "Follow me..."

"Did you hear that?" Rachel gasped.

"Yes," said Kirsty, her eyes wide. "It must be a magic stream!"

"Maybe the stream will lead us to the Yellow Fairy!" said Rachel.

Kirsty's parents had stopped to admire the stream too. "Which way now?" asked Mr Tate.

"Let's go this way," Kirsty said, pointing along the bank.

A kingfisher flew up from a twig. Butterflies as bright as jewels fluttered among the reeds.

"Everything on Rainspell Island is so beautiful," said Kirsty's mum. "I'm glad we still have five days of holiday left!"

Yes, Rachel thought, and five Rainbow Fairies still to find! Ruby the Red Fairy and Amber the Orange Fairy were already safe in the pot-at-the-end-of-the-rainbow.

The girls ran on ahead. As they followed the stream, the sun went behind a big, dark cloud. A chilly breeze ruffled the girls' hair.

Kirsty saw that some of the leaves on the trees were turning brown, even though it wasn't autumn.

"It looks like Jack Frost's goblins are still around," she warned Rachel.

"I know." Rachel shivered. "They'll do anything to stop the Rainbow Fairies getting back to Fairyland."

The stream ran through a meadow. A herd of black and white cows were grazing at the water's edge.

"Aren't they lovely?" Kirsty said.

Suddenly the cows ran off towards the other end of the field.

Rachel and Kirsty looked at each other in surprise. What was going on?

There was a loud buzzing noise. A small angry shape came whizzing through the air, straight towards them!

Rachel almost jumped out of her skin. "It's a bee!"

"Run!" Kirsty cried.

Rachel tore through the meadow with Kirsty beside her, their feet pounding the grass.

"Keep running, girls," called Mr Tate, catching up with them. "That bee seems to be following us!"

Rachel glanced back. The bee was bigger than any
bee she'd ever seen.

"In here, quick!" Mrs Tate called from the side of the
field. She pulled open a wooden gate.

They all ran through, then stopped to get their breath.

"I wonder who lives here?" Kirsty
said, looking around. They were in a beautiful garden.
A path led up to a thatched cottage with yellow roses
around the door.

Just then, a very strange
creature came out from behind
some trees. It looked like an
alien from outer space!

"Oh!" Rachel and Kirsty
gasped.

The creature lifted its gloved
hands and removed its white helmet to reveal...an old
lady! "Sorry if I startled you," she said, smiling.

"I do look a bit strange in my beekeeper's suit."

Rachel sighed in relief. It wasn't a space alien after all!

"I'm Mrs Merry," the old lady went on.

"Hello," Rachel said. "I'm Rachel. This is my friend, Kirsty."

"And this is my mum and dad," Kirsty added.

Mr and Mrs Tate greeted Mrs Merry.

Mr Tate ducked as the huge bee zoomed past his ear. "Watch out!" he said.

"Oh, it's that hiveless queen again," said Mrs Merry. She flapped her hand at the bee. "Go on, shoo!"

Rachel watched it swoop over a hedge and disappear.

"Why did the bee chase us?" Kirsty asked.

"I don't think she was chasing you," said Mrs Merry. "She was just heading this way because she's looking for a hive of her own. But all of my hives already have queens. Since you're here, would you like to try some of my honey?" she asked.

"Yes please!" said Rachel.

They followed Mrs Merry across the lawn to a table covered with rows of jars.

Each jar was filled with rich golden honey. Dappled sunlight danced over the jars, making the honey glow.

"Here you are," said Mrs Merry, spooning some honey onto a pretty plate.

"Thank you," Rachel said. She dipped her finger into the little pool of honey and popped it into her mouth.

The honey was the most delicious she had ever tasted.

Then she felt it begin to tingle on her tongue. "It tastes all fizzy!" she whispered to Kirsty.

Kirsty dipped her finger into the honey too. "Look!" she said.

Rachel saw that the honey was sparkling with a thousand tiny gold lights. She grabbed Kirsty's arm. "Do you think this means—"

"Yes," said Kirsty. Her eyes were shining. "Another Rainbow Fairy must be nearby!"

"We have to find out where this honey came from!" Rachel said.

"Yes," Kirsty agreed. "Mum? Can we stay here a bit longer, please?"

"As long as it's OK with Mrs Merry," Kirsty's mum replied.

Mrs Merry beamed. "Of course they can stay," she said.

Mr and Mrs Tate decided to carry on with their walk.

"Make sure you come back by lunchtime," Kirsty's mum said.

"We will," Kirsty promised.

"Come along then, girls." Mrs Merry set off across the lawn.

Rachel and Kirsty followed her down the garden. Six wooden hives stood underneath some apple trees.

"Which one did the honey we tasted come from?" Kirsty asked.

Mrs Merry looked pleased. "Did you enjoy it? The honey from that hive tastes especially good at the moment."

"I think we might know why," Rachel whispered to Kirsty.

"Yes," Kirsty agreed. "It could be fairy honey!"

"That's the one," Mrs Merry said, pointing to the bottom of the garden. One hive stood there all alone, beneath the biggest apple tree.

As they drew nearer to the hive, a sleepy buzzing sound drifted up into the air.

"The bees in this hive are very peaceful," said Mrs Merry. "I've never known them to be so happy."

"Can we get a bit closer?" Rachel asked.

"I think it's safe, with the bees so quiet," Mrs Merry decided. "But you had better wear a hood, just in case." She went into a shed and brought out two beekeepers' hoods. "Here you are," she said.

Rachel and Kirsty pulled the hoods over their heads.

It was a bit stuffy inside but they could see out of the fine netting. They moved closer to the hive.

The soft buzzing sounded almost like music.

"We need to open it and have a look," Kirsty

whispered to Rachel.

Rachel nodded.

But they couldn't start searching for the Yellow Fairy with Mrs Merry there.

Kirsty had an idea.

"Could I have a drink of water, please?" she asked.

"Of course you can, dear," Mrs Merry said. She went off towards the cottage.

"Quick!" Kirsty spun round. "Let's open the hive."

Rachel grasped one side of the lid. Kirsty took hold of the other side. It slowly came loose with strings of golden honey stretching down.

"Watch out.
It's very sticky,"
Rachel said.

The girls
laid the heavy lid
carefully on the
ground. Kirsty wiped her fingers on the grass.

"Look!" Rachel whispered.

Kirsty turned to see, and gasped.

A shower of sparkling gold dust shot up out of
the hive, shimmering and dancing in the sunlight.
Fairy dust!

Rachel peered down into the hive. A tiny girl was
sitting cross-legged on a piece of honeycomb, in the
middle of a sea of honey.

A bee lay with its head in her lap while she combed
its silky hair. Several other bees were waiting their
turn, buzzing gently.

"Oh, Kirsty," Rachel whispered. "We've found another Rainbow Fairy!"

The fairy had bright yellow hair. She wore a necklace of golden raindrops around her neck and sparkly golden bracelets on her wrists. Her bright yellow T-shirt and shorts were the colour of buttercups.

"Thank you for finding me!" the fairy called up to them. "I'm Saffron the Yellow Fairy."

"I'm Rachel," said Rachel.

"And I'm Kirsty," said Kirsty.

"We've met two of your sisters already – Ruby and Amber."

Saffron beamed. "You've found Ruby and Amber?" She stood up, gently pushing the bee away.

"Yes. They're safe in the pot-at-the end-of-the-rainbow under the willow tree," Rachel said.

Saffron clapped her tiny hands. "I can't wait to see them again." Suddenly she looked worried. "Have you seen any of Jack Frost's goblins near here?"

"No, not here," Kirsty said. "But there were some by the pot yesterday."

"Goblins are scary," Saffron said in a trembling voice. "I've been safe from them here with my friends the bees."

"It's all right," said Rachel. "King Oberon sent one of his frog footmen to look after you and your sisters."

Saffron looked more cheerful.

A large bee crawled from one of the waxy openings in the honeycomb next to Saffron.

"This is my best friend, Queenie," said Saffron. She put her arms round the bee's neck and kissed the top of her furry head.

Queenie buzzed softly.

"She says hello," said Saffron.

"Hello, Queenie," said Kirsty and Rachel.

Saffron picked up her tiny comb and began to comb Queenie's shiny hair. Another bee buzzed crossly.

"Don't worry, Petal, I'll comb your hair next," Saffron said.

Rachel and Kirsty looked at each other in dismay. Why wasn't Saffron flying out of the hive?

"What if Saffron wants to stay with Queenie and the other bees?" Kirsty whispered.

"Saffron, you have to come with us!" Rachel burst out. "Or Fairyland will never get its colours back!" Kirsty added. "It will take all of the Rainbow sisters to undo his spell."

"Yes, of course! We have to break Jack Frost's spell!" Saffron cried. She jumped to her feet and picked up her wand.

Suddenly an icy wind sprung up. Something crunched under Kirsty's feet. The grass was covered with frost!

Rachel shivered as something soft and cold brushed against her cheek. A snowflake in summer? "What's happening?" she cried.

"Jack Frost's goblins must be near," Kirsty said.

Saffron's tiny teeth chattered. "Oh, no! If they find me, they will stop me getting back to Fairyland!"

Kirsty looked at Rachel in alarm. "Quick, we must go!"

Rachel leaned down and carefully lifted the fairy out of the hive. Saffron's golden hair dripped with honey.

"Oh dear, you're really sticky," Rachel said.

Just then Kirsty spotted Mrs Merry coming out of her cottage.

Rachel popped the fairy into the pocket of her shorts.

"Hey! It's dark in here!" Saffron complained.

"Sorry," Rachel whispered. "I'll get you out again in a minute."

Suddenly Kirsty noticed the open hive. "We have to put the top back on!" she said.

Rachel helped her lift it and they put it back just as Mrs Merry came through the trees.

"Here's your drink, dear," said Mrs Merry, holding

out a glass to Kirsty. She had
taken off her strange suit,
and in her other hand she
was carrying a shopping
basket.

"Thank you very much,"
Kirsty said.

"Now, you girls stay as long
as you like," said Mrs Merry.
"I've just remembered I must go and buy some fish
for my cat."

Rachel watched the old lady go towards the garden
gate. Then she slipped her hand into her pocket. "You
can come out now," she said to Saffron.

The fairy was covered with grey fluff from Rachel's
pocket. "Achoo!" she sneezed. She brushed crossly at the
bits of fluff clinging to her wings. "I won't be able to
fly!" she wailed.

"We need to clean you up," Rachel said. "But we'll have to be quick, in case the goblins find us." Kirsty spotted a bird bath filled with clear water.

"We could use that."

"Just what we need," Rachel agreed. She carried Saffron over to the bird bath. Saffron fluttered on to the edge of the bath, put down her wand and dived in. *Splash!*

The water fizzed and turned bright yellow. Lemony-smelling drops shot everywhere.

Sparkling clean, Saffron zoomed up into the air to dry.

"That's better!" she cried.

Her wings flashed like gold in the sun as she swooped onto Rachel's shoulder.

"Goodbye, Queenie!" Saffron called.

Queenie looked out of the entrance to the hive. Her feelers drooped sadly as she waved a tiny leg and buzzed goodbye.

As they headed into the woods, Saffron gave a cry and flew up into the air. "Oh, no!" she gasped. "I've left my wand beside the bird bath!"

Rachel looked at Kirsty in dismay. "We'll have to go back," she said.

"Yes," Kirsty agreed. "We can't leave a fairy wand lying about.

It would be terrible if the goblins found it."

"Oh, dear... Oh, dear..." Saffron murmured. She fluttered anxiously above them as they went back along the path. Rachel paused at the gate.

There was
no sign of any
goblins.

They ran
through the
apple trees,
straight to
Queenie's hive.
Suddenly an
icy blast made them all shiver. They gazed around in
alarm. Icicles hung from the apple trees, and the lawn
was white with frost. The goblins had arrived!

Saffron gave a cry of horror.

An ugly, hook-nosed goblin jumped up on top of
Queenie's hive. He was holding Saffron's wand!

"Give me back my wand!" Saffron demanded.

"Come and get it!" yelled the goblin. He leaped off
the hive and ran towards the garden gate.

Kirsty gasped as another goblin jumped down from the apple tree. Splat! He landed on the frosty grass and set off at a run.

"Catch!" The goblin threw the wand to his friend. It flew through the air, shooting out yellow sparks.

The other goblin reached up and caught the wand. "Got it!"

Just then, Queenie flew out of the hive. All the other bees swarmed behind her in a noisy cloud.

With Queenie in the lead, the bees formed into an arrow shape and surged after the goblins.

"Be careful, Queenie!" pleaded Saffron.

The goblin shook Saffron's wand at Queenie.

"Go away!"

More yellow sparks shot out of the wand. One of the

sparks hit Queenie's wing. Queenie wobbled in mid-air. Then she buzzed and flew at the goblin again.

"Help!" The goblin ducked and dropped the wand.

"Butterfingers!" grumbled the other goblin, scooping it up.

"They're getting away!" Kirsty said in dismay.

"No, they're not!" Rachel cried. The cloud of bees shot across the garden and the goblins disappeared under an angry, black cloud.

"Get off me!" spluttered the goblin with the wand. He tried to brush the bees away, but tripped over his feet. As he fell, he bumped into the other goblin. They tumbled in a heap, dropping the wand on to the grass.

"That was your fault!" complained one of the goblins.

"No, it wasn't!" snapped the other one.

Queenie zoomed over and picked up the wand. She carried it to Saffron, who was standing on Rachel's hand.

Saffron took her wand from Queenie and waved it in the air. A fountain of fluttering yellow butterflies sparkled around them.

"My wand is all right!" Saffron cried joyfully.

"Look! The goblins are going," Kirsty said.

The bees had chased the goblins to the end of the garden. Still arguing, they ran across the fields.

As the grumbling voices faded away, the icy wind dropped. The sun shone warmly and the frost melted. The bees streamed back and flew around Rachel and Kirsty, buzzing softly.

"Thank you, Queenie!" Saffron hugged her friend.

Suddenly Queenie wobbled and tipped sideways. Rachel cupped her hands, worried that Queenie would roll off.

"I think she might be hurt," Saffron said.

She knelt down and looked closely at Queenie. "Oh, no!" she gasped. "She's torn her wing!"

"Can you mend Queenie's wing with magic?" Kirsty asked.

Saffron shook her head. "Not on my own. But Amber or Ruby might be able to help me.

We must take Queenie to the pot-at-the-end-of-the-rainbow!"

Rachel and Kirsty hurried into the woods. Saffron flew behind them, her rainbow-coloured wings shimmering.

Kirsty went over and parted the branches of the willow tree. A large, green frog hopped out from behind the black pot.

"Bertram!" Saffron flew down and hugged him. "I'm so glad you're here!"

Bertram bowed. "Hello, Miss Saffron. Miss Ruby and Miss Amber will be delighted to see you."

Suddenly a shower of red and orange fairy dust shot up out of the pot, followed by Ruby and Amber.

"Saffron!" Ruby shouted.

"It's good to have you back," Amber called happily, doing a backflip.

The air around the fairies fizzed with red flowers,

orange bubbles and yellow butterflies.

Ruby flew on to Kirsty's shoulder. "Thank you, Rachel and Kirsty," she said. She spotted Queenie sitting on Rachel's hand. "Who is this?"

"This is Queenie," Saffron explained. "She helped me get my wand back. But one of the goblins hurt her wing. Can you help?"

Amber frowned. "I could mend Queenie's wing if I had a fairy needle and thread," she said. "But I don't have any here on the island."

Rachel remembered something. "Kirsty! What about the magic bags that the Fairy Queen gave us?"

Kirsty took out her bag. When she opened it a cloud of glitter shot up into the air.

"There's something inside," Kirsty said. She drew out  a tiny, shining needle, threaded with fine spider silk. She held it out to Amber.

"Perfect!" Amber said.

She carefully wove the needle in and out of the tear. The row of stitches glowed like tiny silver dots.

Queenie buzzed softly and flapped her wings. Then she zoomed into the air. Her wing was as good as new!

"You have been such a good friend to Saffron, you must stay with us," said Amber, flying up and hugging the bee.

"Yes!" Ruby agreed. "Please come and live with us in the pot."

Queenie flew down and buzzed in Saffron's ear.

"She says she would love to," said Saffron. "There is a hiveless queen in Mrs Merry's garden who will take care of her bees." Then her face fell. "But what about our sisters? They are still trapped!"

"Don't worry," Kirsty said. "We'll find them soon."

"Yes, we will," Rachel agreed. "Nothing will stop us finding all the Rainbow Fairies!"

Fern
the Green
Fairy

Fern the Green Fairy

"Oh!" Rachel gasped. "What a perfect place for a picnic!"

"It's like a secret garden," Kirsty said, her eyes shining.

They were standing in a large garden. Roses grew around the trees, and marble statues stood half hidden by trailing ivy. Right in the middle of the garden was a crumbling stone tower.

"There was a castle here once called Moonspinner Castle," Mr Walker said. "All that's left is the tower."

"It's just like Rapunzel's tower," Kirsty said. "I wonder if we can get up to the top?"

"Let's go and see!" Rachel said. "Can we, Mum?"

"Off you go," smiled Mrs Walker. "We'll have our picnic when you come back." Rachel and Kirsty rushed over to the door in the side of the tower.

Kirsty tugged at the heavy iron handle. But the door was locked.

"That's a shame," Rachel said.

Kirsty sighed. "Yes, I was hoping Fern the Green Fairy might be here. We have to find her today!"

"Fern," Rachel called in a low voice. "Are you here?"

Here... Here... Here...

Her words echoed off the stones.

Kirsty gasped. "Rachel, look at the ivy!"

Glossy green leaves grew thickly up the tower, but in

 one place the stones were bare, in the shape of a perfect circle.

"It's just like a fairy ring!" Rachel said. She ran round the tower to take a closer look, and

almost tripped over the lace of one of her trainers.

"Careful!" Kirsty said, grabbing Rachel's arm.

Rachel sat down on a mossy stone to retie her shoelace. "There's green everywhere," she said. "Fern must be here."

"We'd better find her quickly then," Kirsty said. "In case Jack Frost's goblins find her first!"

"Where shall we start looking?" Rachel asked, standing up again.

Kirsty laughed. "You've got green stuff all over you!" she said.

Rachel twisted round to look. The back of her skirt was green and dusty. "It must be the moss," she grumbled, brushing it off.

The dust flew up into the air, sparkling in the sun. As it fell to the ground, tiny green leaves appeared and the smell of freshly cut grass filled the air.

Rachel and Kirsty turned to each other. "It's fairy dust!" they gasped.

They walked all round the tower, looking under bushes and inside flowers. But the Green Fairy was nowhere to be found.

Rachel felt very worried. "You don't think the goblins have caught her, do you?"

"I hope not," replied Kirsty. "I'm sure Fern was here, but now she's somewhere else."

She looked down at the tiny leaves. Some of them had begun to flutter across the garden. "I know, let's follow the fairy dust."

The leaves floated over to a path that led into a beautiful orchard.

"It's a magic trail!" Rachel breathed.

They set off along the path, which twisted and turned through the trees.

Suddenly the path opened out into a large clearing. Thick, green hedges loomed above them, their leaves rustling softly.

"It's a maze!" Kirsty cried.

"Look!" Rachel said. "The fairy trail goes right into the maze!"

"We'll have to follow it," Kirsty said bravely.

They followed the floating fairy leaves through the entrance. Kirsty felt a bit scared as the fairy dust led them first one way, then another. What if the trail ran out and they got lost in the maze?

They turned
another corner and
found themselves in
the very centre of
the maze, next to
a pretty nut tree. The
fairy dust led right to the bottom of the tree.

"Fern must be here!" Rachel said.

"Yes, but where?" Kirsty said, looking round.

Tap! Tap! Tap!

"What was that?" Rachel gasped.

Tap! Tap! Tap!

Kirsty pointed at the nut tree. "It's coming from over
there."

"I hope it isn't a goblin trap," Rachel whispered.

Tap! Tap! Tap!

Rachel and Kirsty walked right round the tree. At
first they couldn't see anything unusual.

Then Rachel noticed something strange. There was a small knot halfway up the trunk – and it was covered by a glass window!

Kirsty touched the window. It was cold and wet. "It's not glass," she whispered. "It's ice!"

Suddenly, something moved behind the icy window. Kirsty could just make out a tiny girl dressed in glittering green.

"Rachel, we've found her!" she said. "It's Fern the Green Fairy!"

Fern waved to the girls through the sheet of ice. Her mouth opened and closed, but Rachel and Kirsty couldn't hear what she was saying. The ice was too thick.

"She must be freezing in there," Rachel said. "We've got to get her out."

"We could smash the ice with a stick," said Kirsty. Then she frowned. "But Fern might get hurt."

Rachel thought hard for a moment. "We could melt the ice," she said.

"How?" Kirsty asked, feeling very worried.

"Like this," Rachel replied.

She reached up and pressed her hand against the window. Kirsty did the same.

The ice felt freezing cold, but they kept on pressing with their warm hands.

Soon, a few drops of water began to trickle down the window.

"It's melting!" Rachel said. She gently poked the window with her finger and the ice began to crack.

"Don't worry, Fern," cried Kirsty. "You'll be out of there very soon!"

With a crack, the ice split open. A flash of sparkling fairy dust shot out.

And then Fern the Green Fairy pushed her way out of the window, her wings fluttering limply. She wore a bright green top and stretchy trousers, decorated with pretty leaf shapes. She had green pixie boots, and earrings and a pendant that looked like little green leaves. Her brown hair was tied in bunches, and her emerald wand was tipped with gold.

"Oh, I'm s-s-so c-c-cold!" the fairy gasped. She floated down to rest on Kirsty's shoulder.

"Let me warm you up," said Rachel. She scooped the fairy up in her hands and blew gently on her.

Fern stopped shivering, and her wings straightened out. "Thank you," she said. "I feel much better now."

"I'm Rachel and this is Kirsty," Rachel said. "We're here to take you to the pot-at-the-end-of-the-rainbow."

"Ruby, Amber and Saffron are waiting for you," Kirsty added.

Fern's green eyes lit up. "They're safe!" she exclaimed. "That's wonderful!" She flew off Rachel's hand and twirled joyfully in the air. "But what about my other sisters?"

"Don't worry, we're going to find them too," Kirsty told her.

"How did you get stuck behind the ice window?"

"When I landed on Rainspell Island, I got tangled up in the ivy on the tower," Fern explained. "I untangled myself, but then Jack Frost's goblins chased me. So I ran into the maze and hid in the nut tree. But it was raining, and when the goblins went past, the rainwater turned to ice. So I was trapped."

Rachel shivered. The sun had disappeared behind a cloud, and there was a sudden chill in the air. "It's getting colder," she said.

"The goblins must be close by!" Kirsty gasped.

Fern nodded. "Yes, we'd better go to the pot at once," she said. "You know the way, don't you?"

Rachel and Kirsty looked at each other.

"I'm not sure," Kirsty said. "Do you know, Rachel?"

Rachel shook her head. "We'll have to follow the fairy trail back to the start of the maze."

Kirsty looked around.

"Where is the fairy trail?"

An icy breeze was blowing, and the green fairy leaves were drifting away.

"Oh no!" Kirsty gasped.

"What are we going

to do now?"

Suddenly they heard the sound of heavy footsteps coming through the maze.

"I know that fairy is in here somewhere," grumbled a loud, gruff voice.

"Goblins!" whispered Rachel in dismay.

Rachel, Kirsty and Fern listened in horror as the goblins came closer. As usual, they were arguing with each other.

"Come on!" snorted one goblin. "We can't let her get away again."

"Stop bossing me about," whined the other one.

"Let's hide in the tree," Fern whispered to Rachel and Kirsty. "I'll make you fairy-sized, so we can all fit under a leaf."

Quickly she sprinkled the girls with fairy dust. Rachel and Kirsty gasped as they felt themselves shrinking, down and down.

Fern took the girls' hands. "Let's go," she said, and the three of them fluttered up to a branch. Fern heaved up the edge of a leaf, which was as big as a tablecloth, and they all crept underneath.

A moment later, the goblins rushed into the clearing

"Where can that fairy be?" grumbled one of them. "I know she came this way!"

"How are we going to get back to the pot?" Rachel whispered to Fern.

Fern pointed past them. "Don't worry! I think I know someone who can help us!"

Rachel and Kirsty turned to look. A furry, grey face was peeping round the tree trunk. It was a squirrel.

"Hello," Fern called softly.

The squirrel jumped and hid behind the trunk. Then he peeped out again, his dark eyes curious.

"Maybe he'd like a hazelnut?" Kirsty suggested.

There was a big, shiny nut growing right next to her. She wrapped her arms around it, but she couldn't pull it off the twig.

Rachel and Fern came to help. All three of them tugged at the nut until it came off the branch.

Fern held it out to the squirrel. "Mmm, a yummy nut!" she said.

The squirrel ran lightly along the branch. He took the hazelnut and held it in his front paws.

"What's your name?" asked Fern.

"I'm Fluffy," squeaked the squirrel, between nibbles.

"I'm Fern," said the fairy. "And these are my friends, Rachel and Kirsty. Will you help us get away from the goblins?"

"I don't like goblins," Fluffy squeaked

"We won't let them hurt you," Fern promised. "Can you give us a ride on your back out of the maze? You can jump from hedge to hedge much better than we can!"

"Yes, I'll help you," Fluffy agreed, finishing the last piece of nut.

Rachel, Kirsty and Fern climbed onto the squirrel's back. It was like sinking into a big, soft blanket!

"This is lovely," said Fern, snuggling down. "Let's go, Fluffy!"

Rachel, Kirsty and Fern clung tightly to Fluffy's fur as he jumped out of the tree, right over the goblins' heads! He landed neatly on the nearest hedge. The goblins were so busy arguing, they didn't even notice.

Fern leaned forward to whisper in the squirrel's ear. "Well done, Fluffy. Now the next one!"

Rachel gulped when she saw how far away the next hedge was. "Maybe Fluffy needs some fairy magic to help him," she said.

"No, he doesn't," Fern replied, her green eyes twinkling. "He'll be fine!"

Fluffy leaped into the air and landed safely on top of the next hedge. Rachel and Kirsty grinned at each other. This was so exciting! The squirrel went so fast, it wasn't long before they had left the goblins far behind.

"Now which way do we go?" Fern said as Fluffy reached the edge of the maze.

"This isn't the way we came in," Rachel said. "I don't know the way to the pot from here. Do you, Kirsty?"

Kirsty didn't know either. But she had an idea. "What about looking in our magic bags?"

Fluffy scrambled down to the ground, and Rachel, Kirsty and Fern climbed off his back.

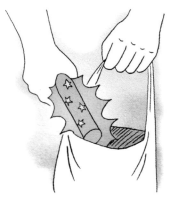

Kirsty opened her rucksack and looked inside. One of the magic bags was glowing with a silvery light.

She pulled out a thin, green tube, covered with sparkling gold stars.

"It looks like a firework," Rachel said. "That's not much use, is it?"

"It's a fairy firework!" said Fern. "We can shoot it into the sky, and my sisters will see it from the pot. Then they'll know we need help."

"But won't the goblins see it too, and know where we are?" said Rachel.

"We've got to take the risk," Fern said.

Kirsty stuck the firework into the ground, then she and Rachel moved away. Fern hovered over the firework.

She touched the top with her wand and quickly flew back to the girls.

With a loud fizz the firework shot upwards, trailing bright green sparks behind it. It climbed higher and higher, until it burst in a shower of emerald stars. The stars spelt out the words

HELP
WE'RE LOST

Rachel and Kirsty wondered what was going to happen. How could the fairies come to their rescue?

They weren't supposed to leave the clearing where the pot was, in case the goblins found them. Suddenly, there was a rustle of leaves behind them.

"Did you see that fairy firework?" shouted a loud voice. "It came from over there!"
Rachel and Kirsty stared at each other in alarm. The goblins were on their trail!

"Don't worry," Fern said. "My sisters will send help quickly."

Rachel spotted a line of golden sparkles twinkling through the fruit trees. "What's that?" she whispered.

"Is it goblin magic?" Kirsty asked anxiously.

Fern shook her head. "They're fireflies! My sisters must have sent them to show us the way back to the pot."

Suddenly there was another shout from inside the maze. "Look at those lights!"

"The goblins have spotted the fireflies!" Rachel gasped.

"Quick, Fluffy!" Fern said, as they climbed onto the squirrel's back again. "Follow the fireflies!"

The golden specks danced away through the trees. Fluffy scampered after them, just as the goblins dashed out of the maze.

"There's the fairy!" one of them shouted. "Stop that squirrel!"

Rachel, Kirsty and Fern clung to Fluffy's fur as the squirrel scrambled up the trunk of the nearest tree.

He was just about to jump across to the next tree, when someone called to them from below.

"Hello!"

"Who's that?" Rachel asked. She, Kirsty and Fern peered down at the ground.

A hedgehog was standing at the foot of the tree. "The animals in the garden would like to help get back to the pot," he called.

"Oh, thank you," Fern replied. Then she gasped as the goblins appeared among the trees.

"Where's that squirrel gone?" one of them yelled.

Fluffy leaped across to the next apple tree. The goblins roared with rage and dashed forward. At that very moment, the hedgehog curled himself into a ball and rolled into their path. He looked like a prickly football.

"OW!" both goblins howled. "My toes!"

Rachel and Kirsty laughed as the goblins jumped around holding their feet.

"Hooray for Hedgehog!" the girls shouted.

As Fluffy jumped from one fruit tree to the next, the firefly lights behind them began to go out.

"Hey! Who turned off the lights?" wailed one of the goblins.

"Which way are we supposed to go?"

"How do I know?" snapped the other goblin. Their voices were getting fainter now as Fluffy hurried on.

"Thank you, fireflies," called Fern, waving at the last few specks of light. "Now we need to find a way to the orchard wall."

"I can help you," a small voice whispered.

A fawn was standing at the bottom of the tree.

She stared up at them with big, brown eyes.

"I can show you a short cut."

She trotted off through the trees.

Fluffy leaped from branch to branch above the little deer's head.

Rachel could hardly believe she was riding on a squirrel's back, being shown the way to the pot-at-the-end-of-the-rainbow by a fawn!

A few moments later they reached the wall which ran round the orchard. On the other side of the wall was a meadow, and beyond that a wood.

"Look!" Rachel shouted. "That's where the pot is!"

"Thank you!" Kirsty and Rachel called to the baby deer. She blinked her long eyelashes at them, and trotted away.

A blackbird hopped over to them, his head on one side. "I'm here to take you to the pot-at-the-end-of-the-rainbow," he chirped.

"All aboard!"

Fluffy looked sad as Fern, Rachel and Kirsty slid off his back and climbed onto the blackbird. His feathers felt smooth and silky after Fluffy's fur.

"Goodbye, Fluffy!" called Rachel. She felt sad to leave their new friend behind.

"Look for the big weeping willow tree," Rachel told the blackbird as he swooped across the meadow.

The blackbird landed in the clearing near the willow tree.

"Who's there?" croaked a stern voice. A plump, green frog hopped out from under the tree.

"Bertram, it's me!" Fern called. She waved her wand, and Rachel and Kirsty shot up to their normal size.

"Miss Fern!" Bertram said joyfully. "You're back!"

"Thank you for sending the fireflies," Fern said, giving the frog a hug.

"We saw the firework in the sky," Bertram explained, "so we knew you were in trouble. You'll be safe here," he added.

Rachel and Kirsty pulled aside the long branches to find the pot.

Suddenly a fountain of red, orange and yellow fairy dust whooshed out. Ruby, Amber and Saffron flew into the air with a queen bee behind them.

"Fern!" Ruby called. "It's so good to see you!"

Rachel and Kirsty beamed as the fairies hugged each other. The air fizzed and popped with red flowers, green leaves, tiny, yellow butterflies and orange bubbles.

"We've really missed you," said Saffron. Beside her, the bee nudged her with a tiny feeler. "Oh, sorry, Queenie," said Saffron. "This is my sister, Fern."

"How did you get back so quickly?" asked Amber.

"Our woodland friends helped us," Fern said. "Especially Fluffy the squirrel." She sighed. "It was a shame we had to leave him behind."

"Who's that then?" Ruby asked, pointing at a tree.

Fluffy was peeping out from behind the trunk.

"Fluffy!" Fern flew over and hugged him. "What are you doing here?"

"I wanted to make sure you got back to the pot safely,"
Fluffy explained shyly.

"Would you like to stay with us?" asked Amber.

"Yes, please," squeaked Fluffy.

Fern fluttered onto Rachel's shoulder. "We'll see you again soon, won't we?"

"Yes, of course," Rachel promised.

"And there's only three Rainbow Fairies left to find!" Kirsty added with a grin, before she took Rachel's hand and they ran out of the clearing.

Sky
the Blue
Fairy

Sky the Blue Fairy

"The water's really warm!" laughed Rachel. She was sitting on a rock, swishing her toes in a rock pool. Her friend Kirsty was looking for shells nearby.

"Mind you don't slip!" called Mrs Tate. She was sitting on the beach with Rachel's mum.

"OK, Mum!" Kirsty yelled back. As she looked down at her bare feet, a patch of green seaweed began

to move.

There was something blue and shiny underneath the seaweed.

"Rachel!" she shouted.

Rachel went over to Kirsty. "What is it?" she asked.

Kirsty pointed to the seaweed. "There's something blue under there," she said. "I wonder if it's…"

"Sky the Blue Fairy?" Rachel said eagerly.

The seaweed twitched.

"Maybe the fairy is all tangled up," Rachel whispered. "Like Fern when she landed on the ivy in the tower."

Fern was the Green Rainbow Fairy. Rachel and Kirsty had already found Fern and her sisters Ruby, Amber and Saffron.

Suddenly a crab scuttled out from under the seaweed. It was bright blue and very shiny. It didn't look like any of the other crabs on the beach.

Kirsty and Rachel smiled at each other. This must be more of Rainspell Island's special magic!

"Fairy in trouble!" the crab muttered. His voice sounded like two pebbles rubbing together.

"Did you hear that?" Rachel gasped.

The crab stopped and peered up at the girls with his little stalk eyes. Then he stood up on his back legs.

"What's he doing?" Kirsty said.

The crab pointed his claw towards some rocks. He scuttled away a few steps, then came back and looked

up at Rachel and Kirsty again.

"I think he wants us to follow him," Rachel said.

"Yes! Yes!" said the little crab, clicking his claws. He set off sideways across a large flat rock.

Kirsty turned to Rachel. "Perhaps he knows where Sky is!"

"I hope so," Rachel replied.

The crab scuttled across a stretch of sand.

"Rachel, Kirsty, it's nearly lunchtime!" called Mrs

Walker. "We're going

back to Dolphin

Cottage."

Kirsty looked at

Rachel in dismay.

"But we have to

stay here and look for

the Blue Fairy. What shall we do?"

The crab jumped up and down, kicking up tiny puffs

of sand.

"Follow me, follow me!" he said impatiently.

"Could we have a picnic here instead, please?" Rachel

called back.

Mrs Walker smiled. "Of course!

I'll pop back to the cottage

with Kirsty's mum and fetch

some sandwiches."

"We'd better hurry," Kirsty said to Rachel. "They'll be back soon."

The crab set off again over a big slippery rock. Rachel and Kirsty climbed carefully after him. Rachel saw him stop by a small pool with lots of pretty pink shells.

"Is the fairy in this rock pool?" she asked.

The crab looked into the pool. He scratched the top of his head with one claw, looking puzzled. Then he scuttled away.

"I guess not," Kirsty said.

"What about here?" Rachel said, stopping by another pool. This one had tiny silver fish swimming in it.

The crab shook his claw at them and kept going.

"Not this one either," said Kirsty.

Suddenly Rachel spotted a large pool all by itself. "Let's try that one," she said.

They ran over and looked into the water. The sky was reflected in the pool like a shiny, blue mirror.

The crab scuttled up behind them. When he dipped his claw into the pool, the water fizzed like lemonade.

The crab lifted his claw out of the water. Blue sparkles dripped off it and landed in the pool with a sizzle. The entire pool was shimmering with magic!

"Thank you, little crab," Rachel said. She crouched down and stroked the top of the crab's smooth, shiny shell.

The crab waved one claw at her, then dived into the water. He sank to the bottom and scuttled under some seaweed.

Kirsty peered into the pool. "Can you see the Blue Fairy?"

Rachel shook her head.

Kirsty felt disappointed. "I can't either."

"Do you think Jack Frost's goblins have found her?" Rachel said.

Kirsty shuddered. "I hope not!"

Just then, they heard a sweet voice singing. "With silver bells and cockle shells, and pretty maids all in a row..."

"Do you think it's the little crab?" Rachel whispered.

Kirsty shook her head. "His voice was all gritty."

"Yes," said Rachel. "This sounds more like a fairy!"

"I think the singing is coming from that seaweed," said Kirsty.

Rachel peered into the pool. "Look!" she said.

A huge bubble came bobbing out of the seaweed and floated towards the surface.

Rachel and Kirsty stared in astonishment. There was a tiny girl inside the bubble!

"I think we've found Sky the Blue Fairy!" Kirsty gasped.

The fairy pressed her hands against the sides of the bubble. She wore a short, sparkly dress and knee-high boots the colour of bluebells. Her earrings and hairband were made of tiny stars, and she was holding a silver wand.

"Please help me!" Sky said in a tiny voice like bubbles popping. Suddenly, a cold breeze stirred Rachel's hair. A dark shadow fell across the pool and the glowing blue water turned grey.

Rachel looked up. The sun was still shining brightly. "What's happening?" she cried.

There was a strange hissing, crackling sound.
A layer of frost crept across the rocks

towards them, covering

the beach in a crisp,

white blanket.

"Jack Frost's
goblins must be
very near," Kirsty said.

Ice began to cover the pool.

"Oh, no!" cried Rachel. "Sky's going to be trapped!"

Sky's bubble stopped bobbing. It hung very still, frozen
into the ice. Sky looked very scared.

"We have to rescue her!" Kirsty exclaimed.

"How can we melt
the ice?" Rachel wondered
anxiously.

"Why don't we look in our
magic bags?" said Kirsty.

Rachel frowned. "Oh, no! I've left them in my
rucksack on the other side of the rock pools! I'll run
back and fetch them."

Kirsty blew on her hands to warm them.

"I'll stay here. But hurry!"

"I won't be long," Rachel promised. She scrambled
back over the rocks and onto the sandy beach.
Her rucksack was lying where she'd left it. She took
out one of the magic bags. It was glowing with a soft
golden light. When she opened it, a cloud of glitter
sprayed out.

Rachel slipped her hand into the bag. There was something inside that felt smooth and shiny. It was a tiny blue stone, shaped like a raindrop.

Rachel felt very puzzled. It was pretty, but how could it help?

The blue stone began to glow in her hand, hotter and hotter until it was almost too warm to hold.

As it grew hotter, it glowed fiery red. Rachel grinned. They could use it to melt the ice and set Sky free!

She ran back as fast as she could. But when she reached the frozen pool, Kirsty wasn't on her own any more. Two ugly hook-nosed goblins were skating on the ice!

"Shoo! Go away!" Kirsty shouted at them.

"Go away yourself!" one of the goblins yelled rudely, sliding away from her.

Kirsty tried to grab the other goblin. But he dodged away.

"Can't catch me!" he shouted.

"Hee, hee! The fairy's stuck in the ice!" laughed the other goblin, doing a little twirl.

"We're going to get her out!" Kirsty told him. "We're going to find all the Rainbow Fairies!"

"Oh no, you won't," said the goblin. He stuck out his tongue.

"Jack Frost's magic is too strong," said the other goblin. "Hey, look at me!" He held out his arms and slid across the ice on one foot. But the ice was very slippery. He crashed right into his friend.

Splat!

"Clumsy!" the goblin snapped.

"You should have moved out of the way," grumbled the other one, rubbing his bottom.

The goblins tried to stand up. But their feet skidded sideways and they fell over again.

Rachel saw her chance. She threw the magic blue stone onto the ice.

A shower of golden sparks shot into the air and the stone glowed bright red. A big hole appeared in the centre of the pool.

"Ow! Hot! Hot!" yelled the goblins. They scrambled to the edge of the pool and

rushed away, their big feet slapping on the rocks.

"They've gone!" Kirsty said in relief.

Rachel peered into the pool.

"I hope Sky isn't hurt," she said.

All the ice had melted and the water reflected the blue sky once again. Sky's bubble was floating just below the surface.

Rachel saw Sky sit up inside the bubble
and look around. She looked very pale.

Kirsty put her hand in the water. It was
still warm from the magic stone. Very gently,
she poked her finger into the bubble to burst it.

Pop!

Sky tumbled free of the bubble and swam up to the
surface, her golden hair streaming behind her.

Kirsty leaned over and fished the fairy out.
She felt like a tiny wet leaf. Kirsty put her
on a rock in the sun. "There
you are, little fairy,"
she whispered.

Sky propped herself
up on one elbow.
"Thank you for helping
me," she said weakly. Water dripped from
her hair and her wings, but there were no blue sparkles.

Kirsty frowned. "All the fairies we found before had fairy dust. What has happened to Sky's sparkles?"

"I don't know," said Rachel. "And she's so pale, almost white."

It was true. You could hardly tell Sky's dress was blue at all.

Kirsty bit her lip. "It looks as if Jack Frost's magic has taken away her colour!"

The little crab scuttled out of the water and made his way across the rock to Sky. "Oh dear, oh dear," he muttered. "Poor little fairy."

Sky shivered. "I'm so cold and sleepy," she sighed.

"What's the matter, Sky?" said Kirsty. "Did the goblins get too close to you?"

Sky nodded. "Yes, and now I can't get warm." She curled up in a tiny ball and closed her eyes.

Rachel felt very scared. Poor Sky looked really ill!

"Don't worry," the crab said in his gritty voice. "My friends will help us." He scuttled up to the top of the rock and snapped his claws.

"What's he going to do?" Kirsty wondered. Then she stared in amazement.

Lots and lots of crabs were coming out of the rock pools around them. Big ones, little ones, all different colours.

The blue crab pointed up at the sky, then down at the ground. His friends pattered away in all directions. Their little stalk eyes waved as they prodded their claws into the cracks between the rocks.

"What's going on?" said Rachel.

Kirsty spotted a tiny pink crab tugging and tugging at something. With a gritty crunch, the crab tumbled over backwards. It held a fluffy white seagull feather in its claws. The crab scrambled up again, waving the feather in the air.

One by one, the other crabs searched out more feathers and brought them over to the rock where Sky lay. Very carefully, the blue crab tucked the feathers round Sky.

"They're trying to warm Sky up with seagull feathers!" Kirsty said.

There were so
many feathers
now that Rachel
couldn't see the
fairy at all. Would
the blue crab's idea work? she wondered.

There was the tiniest wriggle in the feather nest. A
faint puff of blue sparkles fizzed up, smelling of
blueberries. One pale blue star wobbled
upwards and disappeared with a pop.

"Fairy dust!" Rachel whispered.

"But there's not very much of it,"
Kirsty pointed out.

There was another wriggle from inside the nest. The
feathers fell apart to reveal the Blue Fairy, her dress still
very pale. She opened her big, blue eyes and sat up.

"Hello, I'm Sky the Blue Fairy. Who are you?"
she said.

"I'm Kirsty,"
said Kirsty.

"And I'm
Rachel," said Rachel.

"Thank you for frightening the goblins away," said
Sky. "And thank you, little crab, for finding all these
lovely, warm feathers." She tried to unfold her wings,

but they were too crumpled. "My poor
wings," said the fairy, her eyes filling
with tiny tears.

"The feathers have helped, but Sky
still can't fly," Kirsty said.

"Maybe the other Rainbow Fairies
can help," Rachel said.

"Do you know where my sisters
are?" Sky asked.

"Oh, yes," said Kirsty. "So far, we've found Ruby,
Amber, Saffron, and Fern."

"They are safe in the pot-at-the-end-of-the-rainbow under the willow tree," Rachel added.

"Could you take me to them, please?" said Sky. "I'm sure they will make me better."

She tried to stand up, but her legs were too wobbly and she had to sit down again.

"Here, let me carry you," Rachel offered. She cupped her hands and scooped up the feather nest with the fairy inside. Sky waved at the little blue crab and his friends. "Goodbye. Thank you again for helping me."

"Goodbye, goodbye!" The blue crab waved his claw. His friends waved too, their little stalk eyes shining proudly.

Kirsty and Rachel glanced at each other as they crunched across the pebbles. The goblins had got closer to Sky than any of the other Rainbow Fairies. And now the Blue Fairy was hardly blue at all!

Rachel and Kirsty hurried into the woods. Rachel carried Sky very carefully. The fairy lay curled in a ball, her cheek resting on her pale hands.

"Here's the glade with the willow tree," Kirsty said when they reached the clearing. The scent of oranges hung in the air, tickling their noses. Rachel looked round and spotted a fairy hovering over a patch of daisies, collecting nectar in an acorn cup.

"Look!" Rachel said. "It's Amber the Orange Fairy."

Amber fluttered over and settled on Rachel's shoulder.

"Hello again!"

Then she saw Sky lying curled in the feathers. "Oh, no! What's happened? I must call the others," she cried. She waved her wand and a fountain of sparkling orange dust shot into the air.

The other Rainbow Fairies fluttered up all over the clearing.

The air sparkled with red, orange, yellow, and green fairy dust. Bubbles and flowers, tiny butterflies and leaves sprinkled the grass.

The fairies clustered around Sky. The Blue Fairy sat up and gave a weak smile, then flopped back into her nest of feathers.

"Why is she so pale?" Saffron asked.

"The goblins got really close to her," Rachel explained. "They froze the pond. Sky was trapped in a bubble under the ice."

Saffron shuddered. "That's terrible!"

Ruby the Red Fairy zoomed into the air. "We must warm Sky up so that her colour comes back. Let's take her to the pot!"

The fairy sisters sped towards the willow tree, their wings flashing. Rachel and Kirsty carried Sky over in her feathery nest.

As Rachel put Sky down beside the pot, a large green frog hopped out.

"Miss Sky!" he croaked.

Sky gave another weak smile. "Hello, Bertram."

"We have to make Sky warm so she gets her colour back," Fern explained.

Bertram looked very worried. "Jack Frost's goblins are so cruel," he said. "You must stay close to the pot, Fairies, so that I can protect you."

"Don't worry, Sky," said Saffron, giving her a hug. "You'll soon feel better."

Sky didn't answer. Her eyes started to close. She was so pale, her arms and legs seemed almost transparent.

"Oh Bertram, what can we do to help Sky?" Fern gasped.

Bertram looked very serious. "I think it's time for you all to try a spell."

Amber frowned. "It might not work with only four of us. Rainbow Magic needs seven fairies!"

"Bertram's right, we have to try," Ruby said. "Quick, let's make a fairy ring."

The Rainbow Fairies fluttered into a circle above Sky. Rachel noticed a black-and-yellow queen bee and a small grey squirrel appear at the edge of the glade. "Queenie and Fluffy have come to watch," she whispered to Kirsty.

Ruby lifted her wand.

"In a fairy ring we fly,

To bring blue colour back to Sky!" she chanted.

The fairies waved their wands. Four different colours
of dust sparkled in the air – red, orange, yellow, and
green. The dust covered Sky in a glittering cloud.

"Something's happening!" Kirsty said. She could see that Sky's short dress and knee-high boots were turning bluer and bluer. "The spell is working!"

Whoosh!

A shimmering cloud of blue stars shot into the air.

"We did it!" cheered Amber, turning a cartwheel in the air.

"Hooray for Rainbow Magic!" cried Ruby.

Sky yawned and sat up. She brushed the feathers away and looked down at herself. Her face lit up. Her dress was blue again!

"My wings feel strong enough to fly now," she said. She flapped them twice, then zoomed into the air.

The Rainbow Fairies clustered round Sky. The air bubbled with fairy dust – red, orange, yellow, green and blue. It was nearly a whole rainbow!

Rachel and Kirsty beamed.

"You won't need these any more!" Fern laughed, tickling Sky with a long, white seagull feather.

"But I think I might know what to do with them!" said Sky. She gathered up the rest of the feathers. "We could put these on our bed. They'll be very warm and soft."

"That's a very good idea," said Ruby.

"Let's have a welcome home feast," said Fern. "With wild strawberries and clover juice."

Amber did another cartwheel. "Yippee! Rachel and Kirsty, you're invited too!"

"Thank you, but we have to go." Rachel looked at her watch. "Our mums will be waiting with our picnic."

"Oh, yes!" Kirsty remembered. She would love to taste some fairy food but she didn't want her mum to be worried. "Goodbye, we'll be back again soon!"

The fairies sat on the edge of the pot and waved to the girls. "Goodbye! Goodbye!"

Sky fluttered beside Rachel and Kirsty as they walked across the glade. Her dress and boots glowed bright blue, and blueberry scent filled the air.

"Thank you so much, Rachel and Kirsty," she said. "Now five Rainbow Fairies are safe."

As they made their way back to the beach, Rachel looked at Kirsty. "Do you think we can find Izzy and Heather in time? The goblins nearly caught Sky today!"

Kirsty smiled. "Don't worry. Nothing is going to stop us from keeping our promise to the Rainbow Fairies!"

Izzy
the Indigo
Fairy

Izzy the Indigo Fairy

"Rain, rain, go away," Rachel Walker sighed.

She stared out of the window of her attic bedroom. Raindrops splashed against the glass, and the sky was full of purply-black clouds.

"And what about Izzy the Indigo Fairy?" Kirsty said. "We have to find her today."

"Remember what the Fairy Queen said?" Rachel reminded Kirsty.

Kirsty nodded. "She said the magic would come to us."

"That's right," Rachel said. "What shall we do while we're waiting?"

Kirsty went over to the bookshelf and pulled one out. It was so big, she had to use two hands to hold it.

"The Big Book of Fairy Tales,"
Rachel read, looking at the cover.

Kirsty grinned. "If we can't
find fairies, at least we can read
about them!"

She was about to turn the first
page when Rachel gasped. "Kirsty, look at the cover!
It's purple. A really deep bluey-purple."

"That's indigo," Kirsty whispered. "Do you think Izzy
could be trapped inside?"

"Let's see!" Rachel said.

Kirsty opened the book. She thought that Izzy might
 fly out of the pages, but there was no
sign of her. On the first page was
a picture of a wooden soldier.
Above the picture were the
words:

The Nutcracker.

"I know this story," Rachel said. "A girl called Clara gets a wooden nutcracker soldier for Christmas. He comes to life and takes her to the Land of Sweets."

On the next page there was a picture of snowflakes swirling through a forest.

"Aren't the pictures great?" Kirsty said. "The snow looks so real."

Rachel put out her hand and touched the page. It felt cold and wet.

"It is real!" she gasped.

Kirsty looked down at the book again.

The snowflakes started to swirl up from the pages, into the bedroom.

Soon the snowstorm was so thick, Rachel and Kirsty couldn't see a thing.

They were swept up into the air by the spinning snow cloud.

Rachel yelled to Kirsty, "Why haven't we hit the bedroom ceiling?"

"Because it's magic!" Kirsty cried.

Suddenly the snowflakes stopped swirling. Rachel and Kirsty were standing in a forest, with their rucksacks at their feet. Trees loomed around them and snow covered the ground.

173

"This is the forest in the picture," Rachel said. "We're inside the book!"

Then she frowned. There was something odd about this snow. She bent down and touched a snowdrift. "This isn't snow," she laughed. "It's icing sugar!"

Kirsty scooped up a handful and tasted it. The icing sugar was cool and sweet.

Rachel could see a pink and gold glow through the trees. "Let's go and see what that is," she said.

They picked up their rucksacks and set off.

Crack!

Rachel nearly jumped out of her skin as a loud noise echoed through the trees.

"Sorry," said Kirsty. "I trod on a twig."

"Wait," Rachel whispered. "I just heard voices!"

"Goblins?" Kirsty whispered back, looking scared.

Rachel listened.

"No, they sound too sweet and soft to be goblins."

They hurried towards the edge of the forest. When they came out of the trees, they saw that the glow was coming from a dazzling pink and gold archway.

"Look!" Rachel gasped. "It's made of sweets!"

The archway was made of pink marshmallows and golden toffees.

Then they heard the voices again. Two people wearing fluffy white coats were chatting to each other as they scooped icing sugar into shiny metal buckets. They had rosy cheeks and pointy ears. They were so busy they hadn't noticed Rachel and Kirsty yet.

"I think they're elves," Kirsty whispered. "But they're the same size as we are. That means we must be fairy-sized – or, at least, elf-sized – again."

"But we haven't got any wings this time," Rachel pointed out.

Suddenly one of the elves spotted them. "Hello!" she called.

"Who are you?"

"I'm Rachel and this is Kirsty," Rachel explained.

"Where are we?" Kirsty asked.

"This is the Land of Sweets," said the first elf. "My name is Wafer, and this is my sister, Cornet."

"We're the ice-cream makers," added Cornet. "What are you doing here?"

"We're looking for Izzy the Indigo Fairy," Kirsty told them. "Have you seen her?"

The elves shook their heads. "We've heard of the Rainbow Fairies," said Wafer. "But Fairyland is far away from here, across the Lemonade Ocean."

"Maybe you should ask the Sugarplum Fairy for help," Cornet suggested. "She lives on the other side of the village."

The elves led Rachel and Kirsty through the archway of sweets.

On the other side of the arch, the sun shone warmly.
Flowers made of strawberry cream grew beneath milk-
chocolate trees. Pink and white marshmallow houses
lined the street, which was paved with boiled sweets.

"Isn't this great?" Kirsty laughed. "It's like being inside
a giant sweet shop!"

"And it all looks yummy!" Rachel
agreed. There were elves hurrying
everywhere. Some had shiny buckets like the ice-cream
makers, and others carried tiny hammers.

There were gingerbread men too, looking very smart
with their bright bow ties and currant buttons. A tiny
pink sugar mouse scampered across the street,
looking very sweet.

Suddenly a cross-looking gingerbread
man hurried out of one of the houses.

"Hello, Buttons," Wafer said.

"What's the matter?"

"Look at my best bow tie!" said the
gingerbread man, holding it out.
"It was red when I hung it out to
dry, and now it's changed colour!"

Rachel and Kirsty gasped. The little bow tie
was bluey-purple!

"Izzy!" they said together.

The ice-cream elves looked puzzled.

"I think this means that Izzy the Indigo Fairy is close
by," Rachel explained.

"We'd better help you find her before she gets into
trouble," Cornet said.

A small elf ran towards them. He had one hand
clapped over his mouth.

"That's our little brother, Scoop," Wafer explained to
Rachel and Kirsty. "Scoop, what are you up to?"

Laughing, Scoop took his hand away from his mouth.
His lips were indigo!

"I had a drink from the lemonade fountain," he giggled. "All the lemonade's turned bluey-purple. It made my tongue tingle, too!"

"That sounds like more Rainbow Fairy magic!" Kirsty said.

"Where's the lemonade fountain?" Rachel asked.

"In the village square," replied Cornet. "Just round the corner."

"Thanks for your help," said Kirsty. She grabbed Rachel's hand and they ran off.

As soon as Rachel and Kirsty rounded the corner, they skidded to a halt. Bluey-purple liquid bubbled up from a dolphin-shaped fountain in the middle of the square.

A crowd of elves and gingerbread men stood round the fountain, all talking at once. They sounded cross.

A swirl of indigo fairy dust shot up from the middle of the crowd. As the dust fell to the ground, it changed into dewberry-scented inkdrops.

Rachel and Kirsty grinned. They had found another Rainbow Fairy!

"Izzy!" Rachel called, as she and Kirsty pushed their way through the crowd. "Is that you?"

"Who's that?" called a cheerful voice.

Izzy was standing next to the lemonade fountain. She had neat blue-black hair and twinkling, dark blue eyes. She was dressed in indigo denim jeans and a matching jacket, covered with spangly patches. Inkdrop-shaped silver earrings hung in her ears, and her wand was indigo, tipped with silver.

"Who are you?" Izzy said. "And how do you know my name?"

"I'm Kirsty, and this is Rachel," Kirsty said. "We've come to take you back to Rainspell Island."

"We've found five of your sisters," Rachel added.

"That's brilliant news!" Izzy cried.

"How did you get to the Land of Sweets?" Kirsty asked.

"The wind blew me down the chimney of Mermaid Cottage, and into the story of *The Nutcracker*," Izzy said.

Before Rachel and Kirsty could say anything else, the crowd started shouting.

"Look what she's done to the lemonade fountain!" grumbled one elf.

"I didn't mean to," Izzy said. "The lemonade looked so yummy,

I had to have a drink. That's when it turned indigo."

"What about my bow tie?" snapped Buttons.

"I was tired," Izzy said. "I borrowed your lovely bow tie to wrap round me while I had a nap."

The crowd started

to mutter again.

"Wait," Rachel said. "Have you heard about Jack Frost's wicked spell?"

The crowd listened while Rachel told them the whole story. When she'd finished, they didn't look cross any more.

"I'm sorry for all the trouble I've caused," Izzy said. "Please can you tell us how to get back to Rainspell Island?"

"The Sugarplum Fairy will help you," said a Jack-in-the-Box. "She lives just past the jellybean fields."

"Come on, then!" Izzy cried. She took Rachel and Kirsty by the hand.

"Good luck!" called everyone.

Rachel, Kirsty and Izzy walked along the road towards the jellybean fields.

Just outside the village was a rock of golden toffee, as tall as a marshmallow house. Elves were tapping the rock with little hammers to break off pieces of toffee. Other elves picked them up and put them into silver buckets.

"That looks like hard work," Kirsty said. "They don't seem to be collecting much toffee at all!"

Rachel peeped into one of the buckets as an elf walked past. Kirsty was right. There were only a few chips of toffee in it.

"Is there something wrong with the toffee?" Izzy wondered.

The elf with the bucket overheard her.

"It's really hard today," he grumbled. "Anyone would think it had been frozen."

"Frozen!" Kirsty said in alarm. "Do you think that means Jack Frost's goblins are here?"

"I hope not," Izzy said.

Just then, there was a loud, rumbling noise and a shout of "Look out!" An enormous wooden barrel was rolling straight towards them!

And two goblins were running behind, grinning all over their ugly faces.

Izzy gave Rachel and Kirsty a push. "Quick! Get out of the way!"

They jumped aside just in time.

Crash!

The barrel smashed right into the toffee mountain and burst open. Lemon sherbet spilled out in a sticky yellow cloud.

"Izzy! Kirsty!" Rachel coughed. "Are you all right?"

"I think so!" Kirsty sneezed. "Atishoo!"

"HELP!"

Kirsty heard Izzy's frightened voice. But she couldn't
see her through the sherbet cloud.

"Help!" Izzy shouted again. "The goblins have got
me!" Her voice was getting fainter.

"Quick, Rachel!" Kirsty gasped. "Have you got our
magic bags?"

Still coughing, Rachel swung her rucksack off her
back. Inside, one of the magic bags was glowing.
Rachel pulled out a folded paper fan. Puzzled, she
opened the fan up.

It was coloured like a rainbow, with stripes of red,
orange, yellow, green, blue, indigo and violet. Rachel
began to flap the fan at the clouds of sherbet.

Whoosh!

A blast of air from the fan
blew all of the sherbet
away.

"This fan is amazing!"
Rachel gasped.

"Look!" shouted Kirsty.

The goblins had tied Izzy's trainers together with
strawberry bootlaces. They were half-dragging, half-
carrying her up the road.

"We've got to save her," Rachel said, folding the fan
and putting it in her pocket.

"I'll go and tell the Sugarplum Fairy," said one of
the elves.

Rachel and Kirsty ran up the road. The goblins had

a head start, but Izzy was wriggling so much that she slowed them down.

The road led through the jellybean fields. Tall green plants stood in rows, each one covered with different-coloured beans. Elves were picking the jellybeans and putting them into baskets.

One of the goblins skidded to a halt. He grabbed a handful of beans from the nearest plant.

The other goblin did the same.

"Yummy!" said the first goblin, stuffing the beans into his mouth.

"They're so greedy, they're stealing the jelly beans!" Rachel panted.

"Yes, but it gives us a chance of catching them up!" Kirsty puffed.

The elves in the field shouted angrily at the goblins. But that didn't stop them. They were picking beans with one hand and holding on to Izzy with the other.

"I've got an idea," Rachel whispered. She lifted up a basket full of beans which had already been picked.

"Look what I've got," she called. "A whole basket full of beans!"

The goblins' eyes lit up.

"Those jellybeans look yummy," Izzy said to the goblins. "I wish I could have one."

"Be quiet," snapped a goblin. He turned to the other goblin. "You hold the fairy while I get the basket."

"No," said the other one. "You'll eat all the beans! You hold the fairy, and I'll get the basket."

"No!" roared the first goblin. "Then you'll eat all the

beans!"

Glaring at each other, both goblins let go of Izzy and ran towards Rachel.

She threw a handful of beans on the ground and backed away.

The goblins bent down to grab the beans. When they stood up again, Rachel threw another handful down the hill, away from  Izzy. While the goblins were busy stuffing themselves, Kirsty rushed over to untie Izzy. "Are you all right?" she asked.

Izzy wriggled her feet. "Yes, thank you!"

Rachel left the basket on the ground and ran over to Kirsty and Izzy. The goblins began squabbling over the rest of the beans.

"Let's get out of here!" Rachel said.

Suddenly there was a gentle flapping noise. Rachel

looked up to see a butterfly with pink and gold wings fluttering above them. On its back sat a fairy with long, red hair.

The butterfly landed on the ground. The fairy climbed off the butterfly's back and smiled at Izzy and the girls. She wore a long green and gold dress and a tiara.

"Welcome," she said. "I am the Sugarplum Fairy." She looked sternly at the goblins. "What are you doing in the Land of Sweets?" she demanded.

The goblins didn't answer. They were too busy groaning and holding their tummies.

"My tummy hurts," moaned one goblin.

"Mine too," whined the other one. "I feel sick."

Izzy grinned at Rachel and Kirsty. "They've eaten too many jellybeans!"

The Sugarplum Fairy looked even crosser. "As you have stolen so many of our delicious jellybeans," she said to the goblins, "you must be taught a lesson."

"Why don't you make them pick jellybeans?" Izzy suggested.

"What a good idea," smiled the Sugarplum Fairy.

The goblins looked horrified at the thought of more jellybeans! Several elves came running out of the jellybean fields. They marched the goblins into the nearest field and handed them empty baskets.

With sulky faces, the goblins started to pick the beans.

"Serves them right for being greedy!" laughed Izzy.

"Please can you help us get back to Rainspell

Island?" Rachel asked the Sugarplum Fairy.

The beautiful fairy nodded.

"We will send you home by balloon!" she said. She waved her wand at the empty bean basket.

Rachel and Kirsty watched in amazement as it grew bigger and bigger.

"There is your basket," said the Sugarplum Fairy.

"But where's the balloon?" said Rachel.

"What pretty flowers," Kirsty said. She took a closer look and laughed. "They're not flowers. They're pieces of bubblegum!"

Rachel felt puzzled. "How is that going to help?"

Izzy grinned, her eyes sparkling. "Leave it to me!" she said.

She pulled one of the bubblegum flowers off the tree, popped it into her mouth and began to chew.

Screwing up her face, she blew a huge, pink bubblegum bubble. She puffed and puffed, and the

bubble grew bigger and bigger. Soon it was the biggest bubblegum bubble Rachel and Kirsty had ever seen!

Izzy took the bubble out of her mouth and tied a knot in the end. "The perfect balloon!" she said. "Now we're ready to go."

Rachel and Kirsty beamed at each other. What a brilliant way to travel back to Rainspell!

The elves working in the jellybean fields, and the elves who had followed Rachel and Kirsty out of the village, helped to tie the bubblegum balloon to the basket. Then Rachel, Kirsty and Izzy climbed inside.

The Sugarplum Fairy waved her wand at the balloon, showering it with gold sparkles.

"The balloon will take you to Rainspell Island," she said.

"Thank you," called Rachel and Izzy.

Kirsty looked round in dismay. "But there's no wind to make us fly!"

Rachel looked at the leaves on the bubblegum tree. Kirsty was right. They weren't moving at all.

The Sugarplum Fairy smiled. "Rachel, don't you remember what you have in your pocket?" she said.

"Of course! The magic fan!" Rachel exclaimed. She took it out of her pocket and flapped it.

Whoosh!

The blast of air lifted the balloon up into the sky.

"Goodbye!" Kirsty called.

"Thank you for all your help," cried Izzy.

As they bobbed higher, Rachel put away the fan.

Big, puffy clouds swirled around the balloon and the wind roared, rocking the basket from side to side. Rachel, Kirsty and Izzy hung on to each other.

All of a sudden, the wind dropped.

Kirsty opened her eyes.

"We're home!" she gasped.

They were back in Rachel's attic bedroom at Mermaid Cottage. The balloon and the basket had vanished. The book of fairy tales was lying on the floor.

"Where's Izzy?" Rachel said.

"I'm in here!" said a cheeky voice. The Indigo Fairy

popped up from Rachel's

pocket. She fluttered into

the air, showering the

room with fairy dust

inkdrops.

Kirsty picked up

the book and found a

picture of the Land

of Sweets.

"It's a shame we didn't get to taste any of the sweets,"

she said.

A puff of icing sugar floated out of the book and a

shower of jellybeans fell on to Rachel's bed.

"They must be a present from the Sugarplum Fairy!"

laughed Izzy.

Rachel and Kirsty each popped a jellybean into their

mouths. They were tiny, but they tasted lovely!

"Yum!" said Izzy, munching a bean. "Can we take some for my sisters?"

Rachel nodded. "Let's go right away," she said, filling her pockets with beans. She looked at Kirsty and smiled. They had rescued another fairy and escaped the goblins once again. They'd even been inside a fairy story in a book. And now there was only one more fairy to find!

Heather
the Violet Fairy

Heather the Violet Fairy

"I can't believe this is the last day of our holiday!" said Rachel.

She watched her purple kite soar in the clear blue sky above the field beside Mermaid Cottage.

"But we still have to find Heather the Violet Fairy!" Kirsty reminded her.

Rachel felt the kite tug on its string. Something violet and silver flashed at the end of its long tail. "Look!" she gasped.

"What is it?" Kirsty said.

"Do you think it's a fairy?"

"I'm not sure," Rachel said, winding in the string.

As the kite bobbed
towards them, Kirsty saw
that a long piece of violet-
coloured ribbon was tied to its tail.

"It has tiny silver writing on it," Rachel said.

Kirsty crouched down to look closer. "It says, 'Follow me'."

Suddenly the ribbon was lifted up by the breeze. It
fluttered across the field.

"It must be leading us to Heather!" Kirsty said.

"Mum, is it OK if we go exploring one last time?"
Rachel called.

Mrs Walker was talking to Kirsty's mum outside
Mermaid Cottage.

"Of course, if Kirsty's mum agrees," Mrs Walker replied.

"Yes, but don't go far," said Mrs Tate. "The ferry leaves
at four o'clock."

"We'll have to hurry!" Rachel whispered to Kirsty.

They ran through the grass, following the ribbon.

Suddenly it vanished behind a hedge.

Rachel and Kirsty squeezed through the branches.
Luckily the leaves weren't too prickly. On the other side
they found a path, and a gate. There was a sign on the
gate, in purple paint, saying: SUMMER FAIR TODAY!

The girls went through into a pretty garden.
Candyfloss and ice-cream stalls stood at the edge of
a smooth green lawn.

There were people everywhere, chatting and laughing.

Kirsty spotted the ribbon
fluttering towards a merry-
go-round at the far end of
the lawn. It wrapped itself
round the golden flagpole
and danced in the breeze
like a tiny flag.

"It must be leading us
to the merry-go-round!"
Kirsty said.

The merry-go-round was as pretty as a fairy castle.
Rachel stared with delight at the wooden horses on
their shiny golden poles.

"Hello there!" called a friendly voice. "I'm Tom
Goodfellow. Do you like my merry-go-round?"

Rachel and Kirsty turned to see an old man with
white hair and a kind smile.

"It's lovely," Rachel said.

"Look, Rachel," Kirsty gasped. "The horses are all rainbow colours! Red, orange, yellow, green, blue, indigo and violet."

The merry-go-round slowed down and the music stopped.

Rachel noticed that the pillar in the centre was decorated with a picture of rainbow-coloured horse galloping along a beach.

"All aboard for the next ride!" Mr Goodfellow called. He smiled down at Rachel and Kirsty. "How about you two?" he asked, his blue eyes twinkling.

"We'd love to have a go!" said Kirsty. "Quick, Rachel.
there are two horse left!" She scrambled on to one of
them. A name was painted in gold on it's bridle.

"My horse is called Indigo Princess," Kirsty said,
stroking the horse's shiny coat.

Rachel climbed on to a pretty horse next to Kirsty's.
It had a lilac-coloured coat and a silver mane. "Mine is
called Prancing Violet."

"Hold tight everyone!" Mr Goodfellow called out.

The music started and the merry-go-round began to
turn. Prancing Violet and Indigo Princess swooped up
and down on their poles.

Rachel laughed as they spun faster and faster.
The garden flashed by, and the flowers and paths
disappeared in a blur. The sounds of music and laughter
faded away.

Rachel's heart skipped. The only horse she could
see was Kirsty's horse, Indigo Princess. And she could

feel Prancing Violet's hooves thudding on the ground
beneath her!

Kirsty felt a breeze tugging at her hair. Indigo
Princess seemed to toss her head and kick up sand as
she galloped along. "This is like riding a real horse!" she
exclaimed.

The horses began to slow down. The beach faded
away, and the sound of music returned. The merry-
go-round came to a smooth halt.

Kirsty patted Indigo Princess's neck as she dismounted. "Thanks for the special ride!" she whispered. Then she turned to Rachel. "This merry-go-round is definitely magical, but where is Heather the Violet Fairy?"

"I don't know," Rachel said. Then she heard the tiniest tinkling laugh behind her.

Rachel turned round. There was nobody there, just the picture on the pillar in the middle of the merry-go-round.

Rachel blinked. There was a fairy riding the violet-coloured horse! She wore a short, floaty, purple dress, long purple stockings, and ballet slippers. Purple flowers were tucked behind her ear.

"Kirsty!" Rachel whispered. "I think I've just found Heather the Violet Fairy!"

"Heather must be trapped in the painting on the pillar!" Kirsty said. "We've got to get her out!"

"But how?" Rachel said. "What can we do with all these people here?"

Just then, Mr Goodfellow clapped his hands. "Follow me, everyone. The clowns are here!"

Everyone cheered and scrambled off the merry-go-round. Rachel and Kirsty were left alone.

"Now's our chance!" Kirsty said.

"Let's use our magic bags," Rachel said.

Kirsty put her hand in her pocket and took out her magic bag. When she opened it, a cloud of glitter fizzed into the air. There was something long and slim inside. It was a tiny golden paintbrush.

Kirsty frowned. "We don't want to paint any more pictures."

"Maybe Heather knows what we can use it for," Rachel said.

"Good idea," Kirsty said. As she bent closer to the picture on the pillar, the brush touched the painted fairy's hand. Suddenly, the whole picture glowed, and the fairy's tiny fingers moved!

"Look!" Rachel gasped. "She's coming alive!"

"The brush is working magic on the painting!" Kirsty whispered.

She began to stroke the brush round the outline
of the fairy. The picture glowed even
brighter.

"That tickles!" said the fairy
with a silvery laugh.

With Kirsty's last stroke, the
fairy sprang out of the painting.
Purple fairy dust shot everywhere,
turning into violet-scented blossom.

"Thank you for rescuing me!" said
Heather. "I'm Heather the Violet Fairy! Do

you know where my Rainbow

sisters are?"

"I'm Rachel, and this is Kirsty,"

said Rachel. "Your sisters are safe in

the pot-at-the-end-of-the-rainbow,

under a willow tree."

Heather did a twirl of delight. "Hooray!"

She landed gently on Kirsty's hand. Kirsty held her out of view until they had run through the garden, past the people watching the clowns.

They ran out of the gate, and down the path that led to the wood. As soon as they reached the clearing, there was a shout from inside the pot. Izzy the Indigo Fairy zoomed out. "Heather, you're safe! Look, everybody! Rachel and Kirsty have found Heather!"

Saffron flew out of the pot on the back of a bumble-bee, followed by the other Rainbow Fairies. The air flashed and fizzed with scented bubbles, flowers and leaves, stars, inkdrops and tiny butterflies. Bertram the frog footman hopped out from behind the pot, beaming from ear to ear.

"We knew you were coming," said Amber the
Orange Fairy, doing a
cartwheel. "I've been
tingly with magic
all morning!"

Rachel and Kirsty held hands and danced in a circle.
They had found all seven Rainbow Fairies!

Ruby the Red Fairy's wings sparkled as she fluttered
down to land on Rachel's shoulder. "Thank you,
Rachel and Kirsty," she said.

"You are true fairy friends," agreed Fern the Green Fairy.

Suddenly Rachel heard a strange crackling sound. She spun round. The pond at the edge of the glade wasn't blue any more. It was white and cloudy with ice!

"Goblins!" cried the fairies.

Izzy's tiny teeth chattered. "B-b-but it can't be. The Sugarplum Fairy kept them in the Land of Sweets!"

Just then, a harsh cackling laugh rang out. The bushes parted, and a tall bony fairy walked into the glade.

Icicles hung from his clothes and there was frost on his hair and eyebrows.

It was Jack Frost!

"So you are all together again!" Jack Frost's voice sounded like icicles snapping.

"Yes, thanks to Rachel and Kirsty," Ruby declared bravely.

"And now we want to go home to Fairyland!" She flew into the air. "Come on, Rainbow Fairies!"

Izzy shot to her sister's side, and turned to face Jack

Frost. She looked very determined.

The other fairy sisters flew to join them, and

they all lifted their wands, chanting together:

"To protect the Rainbow Fairies all,
Make a magic raindrop wall!"

A rainbow-coloured spray shot out of each wand and

a shining wall of raindrops appeared between the fairies

and Jack Frost.

"It will take more than a few raindrops to stop me!"
Jack Frost hissed. He pointed a bony finger at the
shimmering wall.

The raindrops turned to ice. They dropped onto the
frosty grass like tiny glass beads and shattered.

The fairies looked horrified. Saffron and Sky gave a
sob of dismay and Izzy clenched her fists. Fern, Amber
and Ruby hugged each other.

Heather looked as if she was thinking hard. Then she
waved her wand, and cried:

"To stop Jack Frost
from causing trouble,
Catch him in a magic bubble!"

A gleaming bubble popped out of the end of
Heather's wand. It grew bigger and bigger.

Jack Frost laughed, and stretched out his icy fingers.
But before he could do anything, there was a loud
fizzing sound. Jack Frost vanished.

Rachel blinked in surprise.

Heather's spell had
trapped Jack Frost inside
the bubble! The wicked
fairy pressed his hands
against the pale lilac wall,
looking furious.

"Well done, Heather!" Fern
exclaimed. "That was very brave!"

"Quick, everyone. We must get into the pot-at-the-end-of-the-rainbow and magic a rainbow to take us back to Fairyland!" Heather urged.

Rachel and Kirsty held the branches out of the way so that the fairies could fly through.

A squirrel skittered down the trunk.

"Who are you?" Heather asked.

"This is Fluffy," said Fern, stroking the squirrel.

"Fluffy and Queenie will have to go back to their homes now," said Sky.

"We'll come and visit them, won't we?" Fern said. All the fairies nodded.

Fern reached up to give Fluffy one last hug before he scampered off.

Queenie buzzed goodbye as she flew away.

Heather fluttered in front of Rachel and Kirsty. "Would you like to come to Fairyland with us?" Rachel and Kirsty nodded. Heather waved her wand, sprinkling the girls with purple fairy dust. Kirsty felt herself shrinking. The grass seemed to rush towards her. "Hooray! I'm a fairy again!" she cried.

Rachel laughed in delight as wings sprang from her shoulders.

Just then, there was a yell from the giant bubble.

Rachel and Kirsty looked round.

Jack Frost was looking very scared. His face was bright red and drops of

water ran down his cheeks. He was melting!

Sky's wings drooped. "Without Jack Frost, there
will be no seasons. We need his cold and ice to make
winter," she said.

"No winter?" Izzy looked
shocked. "But I love sledging
in the snow and skating on the
frozen river."

"Without winter, how can spring follow?" Amber
said. "What will happen to all the lovely spring
flowers?"

 "And the bees need the flowers
to make honey in summer," Saffron
said sadly.

"And in autumn, the squirrels
find nuts to store for winter," said
Fern. "We have to have all the
seasons. But that won't happen if we

leave Jack Frost trapped in the bubble."

Heather spoke up. "You're right. But most importantly, I feel sorry for Jack Frost. He looks very frightened."

"We have to do something," said Ruby.

"But he might cast another spell!" Kirsty said.

"Even so, we have to help him, don't we?" Amber said. All the other Rainbow Fairies agreed.

Kirsty felt very proud of them. The fairies were being so brave!

Sky hovered over the giant bubble. She whispered her spell so quietly that Rachel and Kirsty couldn't hear the words.

A jet of blue fairy dust streamed out of her wand into the bubble. The dust swirled in a spiral until it filled the whole bubble.

Rachel and Kirsty flew over and peered in.

The fairy dust had turned into huge crystal

snowflakes. The water on Jack Frost's face froze. He had
stopped melting! The wind whipped the snow faster,
spinning Jack Frost in circles.

"Look! He's getting
smaller!" Kirsty
gasped, pointing
to the bubble.

Now Jack Frost was smaller than
a goblin. Then he was smaller
than a squirrel, then even smaller than
Queenie the bee! With a loud POP,
the bubble burst. The wind dropped
and the snow vanished.

At first Kirsty thought Jack Frost had
completely disappeared. Then she saw
a very small glass dome lying on the

grass. There was a tiny figure leaping angrily about

inside the dome, shaking his fists.

"It's a snow dome!" Kirsty said

in amazement.

"And Jack Frost's trapped

inside!"

"Hooray for Sky!" shouted

Rachel. "Now we can take Jack Frost safely back to

Fairyland."

She flew over and picked up the snow dome. It felt

smooth and cold, and it trembled when Jack Frost

leaped about.

Bertram hopped towards Rachel. "I'll take care of

that, Miss Rachel," he said.

"Into the pot, everybody!" shouted Izzy. "It's time to

go back to Fairyland!"

"Yippee!" yelled Amber, doing a backflip in mid-air.

Heather waved her wand and the pot rolled on to its

four short legs. Rachel, Kirsty and all the fairies flew inside. Bertram the frog climbed in too.

It was a bit of a squash, but Rachel and Kirsty were too excited to mind.

"Ready?" Ruby asked.

Her sisters nodded. The seven Rainbow Fairies raised their wands. There was a flash above them, like a rainbow-coloured firework. A fountain of sparks filled the pot: red, orange, yellow, green, blue, indigo, and violet.

And the brightest rainbow Rachel and Kirsty had ever seen soared up into the sky.

With a whoosh, Bertram and the fairies shot out
of the pot, carried on the rainbow like a giant wave.

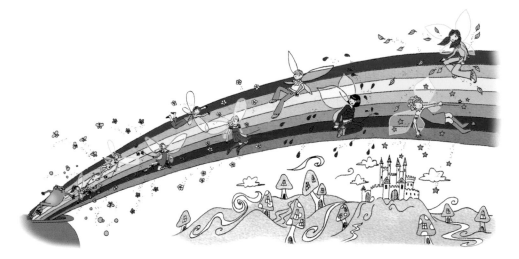

Rachel and Kirsty felt themselves zooming up the
rainbow too. Flowers, stars, leaves, tiny butterflies,
inkdrops and bubbles fizzed and popped around them.

"This is amazing!" Kirsty shouted.

Far below, she could see hillsides dotted with
toadstool houses. It was Fairyland!

All of a sudden, the rainbow vanished in a fizz of fairy dust. Kirsty and Rachel flapped their wings and drifted gently to the ground. Rachel looked around, expecting to see all the colours coming back to Fairyland.

But the hills and the toadstool houses were still grey!

"Why hasn't the colour returned?" Rachel gasped.

One by one, the Rainbow Fairies landed next to them. And Kirsty saw that when each fairy touched the ground, a patch of the greenest green started spreading outwards from their feet.

"Rachel, look!" Kirsty cried. The fairy sisters stood in a circle and raised their wands. A fountain of rainbow-coloured sparks shot up. There was a flash of golden lightning, and it began to rain.

Rachel and Kirsty gazed in delight as tiny glittering raindrops, every colour of the rainbow, pattered down around them. Where they fell, the colour returned, flowing like shining paint across everything in Fairyland.

The toadstool houses gleamed red and white. Brightly-coloured flowers dotted the green hillside with orange, yellow and purple.

On the highest hill, the fairy palace shone softly pink. Music came out as the front doors opened.

"Hurry!" Ruby said. "The King and Queen are waiting for us."

Rachel and Kirsty and the seven fairies flew towards the palace.

Bertram hurried along below them with enormous leaps.

Fairies, elves and pixies rushed out of the palace. "Hooray for the Rainbow Fairies!" they cheered. "Hooray for Rachel and Kirsty!"

Titania and Oberon came out of the palace.

"Welcome back, dear Rainbow Fairies," said Titania.

Bertram bowed. "This is for you, Your Majesty," he said, giving the snow dome to the King.

"Thank you, Bertram," said Oberon.
He looked into the dome. "Now, Jack
Frost," he said sternly. "If I let you out,
will you promise to stay in your icy
castle and not harm the Rainbow
Fairies again?"

Jack Frost scowled and didn't answer.

"Remember that winter still belongs to you," Titania
said.

"Very well," said Jack Frost. "But on one condition."

"And what is that?" asked Oberon.

 "That I'm invited to the next
Midsummer Ball," said Jack Frost.

Titania smiled. "Of course we'll invite
you. You will be very welcome," she
said kindly.

Oberon tapped the snow dome and it cracked
in half. Jack Frost sprang out and shot up to his full

height. He snapped his fingers
and a sledge made of ice
appeared next to him.
Hopping onto it, he zoomed up
into the sky.

"Goodbye. We'll see you at the Midsummer Ball!"
Sky called after him.

Jack Frost looked over his shoulder. A smile
flickered across his sharp face, then he was gone.

The Fairy King and Queen smiled at
Rachel and Kirsty.

"Thank you, dear
friends," said Oberon.
"Without you, Jack
Frost's spell would never have been broken."

"You will always be welcome in Fairyland," Titania
told them. "And wherever you go, watch out for magic.
It will always find you."

The Rainbow Fairies fluttered over to say goodbye.
Rachel and Kirsty hugged them all in turn.
They couldn't help feeling sad that their fairy
adventures were over.

"Here's a special rainbow to take you home!" said
Heather.

The fairies raised their wands one more time. An
enormous shining rainbow whooshed upwards.

"Here we go!" Rachel shouted as she felt herself
being sucked into the fizzing colours.

"I love riding on rainbows!" said Kirsty.

Soon the holiday cottages appeared below them. They landed with a soft bump behind Mermaid Cottage.

"We're back to our normal size," Rachel said, standing up.

"Just in time to catch the ferry!" Kirsty added as they ran round to the front garden.

"There you are," said Rachel's mum. "Did you see that beautiful rainbow? And it wasn't even raining. Rainspell Island is a really special place!"

Kirsty and Rachel shared a secret smile.

"Check your bedroom to see if you've left anything behind," said Kirsty's mum.

"OK," said Kirsty. She dashed into Dolphin Cottage
and went upstairs.

"I'll check mine, too!" Rachel hurried to Mermaid
Cottage and ran up to the attic.

She stopped dead in her bedroom doorway. "Oh!" she
gasped.

In the middle of the bed,
something glittered like a
huge diamond.

It was a snow dome,
full of fluttering fairy dust
shapes.

Rachel scooped up the
dome and dashed next
door.

Kirsty was running
downstairs with a matching
snow dome.

The two friends beamed at each other. "Every time I shake my snow dome or see a rainbow, it will make me think of the Rainbow Fairies," said Rachel.

"Me too!" replied Kirsty. "We'll never forget our secret fairy friends!"

Flora
the Fancy Dress
Fairy

Meet Flora
the Fancy Dress Fairy

When the goblins tried to ruin Rachel and Kirsty's fancy dress party, Flora the Fancy Dress Fairy fluttered straight over to help!

Happiest hobby

Fluttering around Fairyland, wearing new outfits and getting ready for special parties.

Favourite fairy playmate

Polly the Party Fun Fairy.

Yummiest food

Muffins, strawberry ice cream and chocolate cake.

When the queen and king of Fairyland throw a special party, they always ask Flora to create glamorous outfits for everyone attending.

Most trusted magic

Flora only has to wave her wand to create the best party outfit ever!

Wearing a new outfit for the first time is always very exciting!

Favourite colour

Turquoise, the colour of her favourite mermaid outfit.

Personality

Funny, kind and always happy to help.

Fairy outfit

Demi the Dressing-Up Fairy gave her the special mermaid outfit that she loves wearing! Flora's blue bandana top is just the right shade to match her green ballerina shoes. She loves her long curly hair and her sparkly pink tiara of shells.

Goblins one and goblins all,
I summon you to my summer ball!
At McKersey Castle we will meet
To sing and dance and drink and eat!

The reason I am sure is plain.
It's to celebrate my glorious reign.
So on full moon night, to the castle gate,
Come with gifts and don't be late!

Contents

McKersey Castle

"Rachel, look!" Kirsty Tate cried excitedly, pointing through the car window. "There's McKersey Castle!"

Rachel Walker, Kirsty's best friend, stared down the long drive at the huge, greystone castle ahead. It was set on a hill, amid sweeping grounds, and it had two tall turrets, one on either side of the entrance gate.

"It's beautiful," Rachel breathed. Mrs Tate, who was driving, smiled in agreement. "Isn't it the perfect place for a party?" she said. "It was so clever of Lindsay and Robert to choose a castle for their fancy dress ball."

Lindsay was Kirsty's cousin, and she and her husband
were celebrating their tenth wedding anniversary at
McKersey Castle. Kirsty and her parents had been
invited, and Kirsty was allowed to bring a friend, so
Rachel had travelled with the Tates all the way to the
Scottish Highlands.

"It's a ball too," Mr Tate added.

"That'll be fun," Rachel said eagerly. Kirsty nodded.
"Wow!" she exclaimed as they drew closer to the castle.
"There's a moat and a drawbridge!"

"Just like a fairytale castle," Rachel said, smiling at
Kirsty.

Kirsty grinned at her friend. She and Rachel knew a
great deal about fairies, because they'd met them many
times. The girls and the fairies were now the best of
friends, and that was Rachel and Kirsty's very special
and magical secret.

The two girls watched with delight as the car crossed
the drawbridge and came to a stop in the courtyard.

"Look at the battlements." Rachel
said, as she and Kirsty climbed
out of the car.

"I wonder if we're allowed
to go up there."

"Hello!" cried Lindsay,
Kirsty's cousin, rushing out of
the large oak doors with her
husband Robert. She hugged the

Tates one by one. "And you must be Rachel," Lindsay said, giving Rachel a hug too.

"Come inside, everyone."

"Is everything ready for the party tomorrow night?" Kirsty asked as they carried their bags towards the entrance hall.

"Not quite!" Lindsay replied.

"The cake is coming today, and the party planning company who are organising everything are delivering the fancy dress costumes tomorrow. You'll be able to choose your outfits then."

"The other guests are arriving tomorrow too," Robert added, as they stepped into the entrance hall.

Inside the castle, it was cool and welcoming. There were tall arched windows, a flagstone floor, and a suit of armour standing in one corner. Colourful embroidered banners and tapestries hung from the ceiling over the walls.

"I've picked out a special bedroom for you two,"
Lindsay said to Kirsty and Rachel, as Robert led Mr and
Mrs Tate to their room. "Follow me."

Lindsay led the girls up a winding staircase.

"Ta-dah!" she announced, throwing open a small
wooden door.

Rachel and Kirsty gasped with delight when they saw
the huge room with its two canopied beds and pretty
white furniture. One side of the room was taken up with
an enormous window, and after the girls had put their
bags down, they went to look out.

"We're right over the drawbridge!" Rachel cried excitedly.

"This used to be the old gatehouse," Lindsay explained.

"And where does that door by the wardrobe lead?" asked Kirsty.

"Come and see," Lindsay replied.

The door opened onto another narrow staircase which led to the castle battlements.

"Look!" Rachel said, pointing across the hills.

"We're so high, it seems like we can see the whole of Scotland!"

"I gave you that bedroom because I thought you two girls would be great at protecting the castle from intruders," Lindsay joked, her eyes twinkling. "I don't want anything to spoil this party!"

Suddenly, Kirsty spotted a white van approaching the drawbridge. "'McKersey Village Cakes'," she read from the side of the van.

"My cake!" Lindsay cried, hurrying over to the stairs. "I'm dying to see it, girls! It was so difficult to arrange, but a party's no good without a cake, is it?" She grinned at them. "Be careful up here, won't you?"

The girls nodded. "Lindsay's really excited, isn't she?" Kirsty laughed, as her cousin clattered off down the stairs.

"So am I!" Rachel said, smiling, but then she shivered. "Ooh! Did you just feel that blast of icy wind, Kirsty?"

"Yes," Kirsty agreed, frowning.

Rachel's eyes widened. "I can see ice!" she gasped, pointing. "There, all over the steps up to that turret!"

The girls hurried over to investigate the turret to the left of the drawbridge.

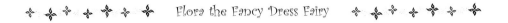

Curiously they began to climb the frozen steps. As they did so, the air got colder and colder. And then, suddenly, Rachel and Kirsty heard a horribly familiar, icy voice.

"Raise my flag to the top of this tower!" it snapped.

Hardly daring to breathe, the two girls peeped round the turret up to the top of the steps. To their utter dismay, standing there, next to a gnarled green goblin, was Jack Frost himself!

Fairies to the Rescue

"Nothing will stop me holding my Icicle Party here tomorrow night," Jack Frost declared, as his goblin servant struggled with the flag. "Certainly not a pesky human fancy dress party!"

Rachel and Kirsty glanced at each other in horror. Jack Frost was planning a party at the castle on the same night as Lindsay and Robert!

"This is the perfect place for my party," Jack Frost continued. "It's miles from anywhere!"

At last the goblin managed to haul the flag to the top of the flagpole. As it unfurled, Rachel and Kirsty saw that it was a picture of Jack Frost wearing a golden crown.

"Now we have to get rid of the humans,"

Jack Frost mused. "We will return to my ice castle immediately, and plan how to ruin this silly fancy dress party before it's even begun!" And with a loud cackle, Jack Frost zoomed away with the goblin on a blast of icy wind.

"They've gone," Rachel said, relieved.

"But they'll be back!" Kirsty pointed out. "And how are we going to stop them ruining Lindsay and Robert's party?"

Rachel thought for a moment. "We could ask the fairies for help," she suggested. "We have our lockets full of fairy dust to take us to Fairyland."

Kirsty nodded eagerly. "Maybe the Party Fairies can
help us," she said, as she and Rachel opened their
lockets.

The girls sprinkled the glittering fairy dust over their

heads, and immediately
found themselves
tumbling through the
air, shrinking into
fairies and surrounded
by dancing rainbows.

As the rainbow
colours drifted away,
Rachel and Kirsty floated
gently to the ground outside the pink Fairyland palace.

"Shall we knock on the door?" Rachel asked. It was
the first time they'd ever arrived in Fairyland without
anyone to meet them.

Kirsty nodded, so Rachel lifted the butterfly-shaped
door-knocker and tapped on the door.
Almost straightaway, Bertram the frog footman
hopped out.

"Hello, girls!" he exclaimed,
looking surprised.
"Welcome to Fairyland
once again."

"Hello, Bertram," said
Kirsty, "Could we see the
King and Queen, please?"
Bertram bowed and took a small
silver bell off the table. He shook it.

"Kirsty and Rachel to see the King and Queen!" sang
out a silvery, chiming voice.

The girls listened in amazement as inside the palace
lots of bells tinkled, passing on the same message from
room to room.

"The King and Queen will see you now!" a message
came tinkling back.

"Follow me to the audience chamber, please," said
Bertram.

The King and Queen were sitting on their glittering
golden thrones when Bertram showed the girls into the
chamber.

It was a large room with a domed ceiling studded
with silver stars.

"This is a pleasant surprise," said King Oberon.

"Do you need our help, girls?" asked Queen Titania kindly.

"Your Majesty, Jack Frost is trying to spoil my cousin's party at McKersey Castle tomorrow," Kirsty explained.

"He wants to hold his own party there instead," added Rachel.

"We are holding our annual costume ball here at the palace tomorrow night," Queen Titania said, frowning.

"Maybe Jack Frost didn't receive his invitation, and that's why he's throwing his own party."

"Can you help us?" asked Kirsty.

"Yes, we know just the fairy to help," declared the King.

The Queen smiled and waved her wand, and a cascade of multi-coloured sparkles streamed out of the open window.

A few moments later, a fairy zoomed in and landed gently on the marble floor. Rachel and Kirsty stared at her. The fairy was dressed as Snow White, in a long red dress, and carried a basket with an apple inside.

"This is Flora the Fancy Dress Fairy," said the Queen.

"Hi, girls!" Flora beamed at them. "How can I help you?"

The girls quickly explained about Jack Frost's nasty plans to ruin Robert and Lindsay's party. Flora shook her head, looking quite annoyed.

"Don't worry," she said firmly, "we won't let Jack Frost spoil the party!"

Goblin Trouble

"We can stop Jack Frost and those naughty goblins from ruining everything," Flora went on, "just as long as they don't get hold of my magic fancy dress items."

"What are they?" asked Kirsty.

"Flora's magic items change all the time," the Queen explained. "Just like Flora's costumes!"

Flora nodded. "At the moment, and for Lindsay's party, my three magic items are a porcelain figurine

in a princess gown, a Red Riding
Hood cape and a black mask
with rainbow-coloured
feathers," she told the
girls.

"The figurine will
make the party food
wonderful, the cape helps
the costumes look good, and
the mask ensures all the guests
have a great time."

"So if the goblins get hold of those three magic things,
they will be able to spoil Lindsay's party?" asked Kirsty
nervously.

"Yes, but luckily Jack Frost and the goblins don't
know what they are!" Flora laughed. "Now, let's hurry
to McKersey Castle and keep an eye on the party
preparations. Just let me change my outfit."

Flora waved her wand over her head, and a shower of turquoise and emerald sparkles drifted down around her. Rachel and Kirsty watched in amazement as the fairy's long, curly hair became a tumble of green and blue ringlets, topped with a tiara of shells. Flora's red dress became a blue bandana top and, best of all, a shimmering, iridescent turquoise skirt which curved up into a beautiful mermaid's tail at her ankles.

"What a gorgeous costume!"
Kirsty breathed.

"Now, be sure to watch
out for any goblin
tricks!" said the King,
as the Queen lifted her
wand to shower them
with fairy magic.

The girls and Flora
nodded as they were swept

up in a cloud of fairy dust. A moment later they found
themselves back on the battlements of McKersey Castle
and Rachel and Kirsty were human-sized again.
Flora looked up at Jack Frost's flag and tutted. Then she
waved her wand and immediately a stream of blue and
green sparkles surrounded the flag. When they cleared,
the picture of Jack Frost had vanished and an L and an
R were intertwined in curly pink letters.

"That's better!" Flora
declared.

Rachel was looking over
the battlements at the
courtyard below. The cake
van was parked there, its back

doors open. But the next second she spotted something
else: goblins!

"There's a group of goblins around the cake van!"
Rachel cried.

"The delivery man must be inside the castle with
Lindsay," said Kirsty.

"I hope he's taken the cake with him."
But as the girls and Flora watched, they saw three
goblins climbing out of the van. They were holding a
large cardboard box which they began to tear apart,
revealing a beautiful three-tiered cake.

"The goblins have got Lindsay's cake!" Kirsty wailed.

"And, look," Rachel added, pointing at another smaller van, parked in the courtyard, with 'Jack Frost's Frosted Delights' written on the side. "They're going to drive away with it!"

Cake Chaos

"We'll get down there more quickly if you're fairy-sized, girls!" Flora said firmly, and, with a swish of her wand and a sparkle of magic, Rachel and Kirsty were fairies again. Immediately, the three friends flew over the battlements and zoomed down to the courtyard.

"Oh, no!" Flora exclaimed as they hovered above the goblins. "My magic figurine is on top of the cake!" Rachel and Kirsty looked closer. On top of the white and  silver icing was a delicate porcelain figure wearing a gorgeous, flowing, yellow dress.

"So if the goblins steal it, then all the party food will be spoilt?" Rachel asked in dismay.

Flora nodded, whizzing down to confront the goblins, with Kirsty and Rachel close behind.

"Put the cake down!" Flora demanded.

One of the goblins poked his
tongue out. "Go away,
pesky fairies!" he
jeered. "We're taking
this cake to Jack
Frost for his party."

Another goblin
grabbed a chunk of
icing from the cake and
flung it at Flora and the girls, so that they had to dodge
quickly out of the way.

The other goblins cackled with glee and immediately
started pulling off chunks of cake and hurling them in
the direction of Flora, Rachel and Kirsty

"Help!" Rachel cried, as a large piece almost hit her.

"They're ruining the cake!" Kirsty gasped.
Frowning, Flora lifted her wand. Suddenly a whoosh of
magic sparkles sent a piece of the cake zooming back

towards the goblin who'd thrown it. It hit him in the
mouth and he recoiled. Then he licked his lips.

"Yum!" he declared. He pulled off another lump of cake,
but this time, instead of hurling it at the girls, he ate it.

"Greedy-guts!" hollered the goblin next to him, but he
stuffed a bit of cake into his mouth too.

"Leave some for us!" the other goblins shouted, and they
also began gobbling chunks of cake.

"Stop!" the biggest
goblin shouted
suddenly. "Jack Frost's
waiting for us. We'd
better put the cake
in the van."

As the goblins
struggled to load the
enormous cake into the back of their van, Flora, Rachel
and Kirsty wondered what they could do to stop them.

JACK FROST'S
FROSTED DELIGHTS

"Oh!" Rachel gasped suddenly. "They'll have to drive over the drawbridge to get out, won't they?"

Kirsty nodded. Then she grinned, catching on. "So if we lift the drawbridge up, they won't be able to leave!" she cried.

"That's brilliant, Rachel!"

The goblins had piled into the van and were already on their way. Quickly, Flora waved her wand and pointed it at the drawbridge.

Instantly, emerald sparks zipped towards the heavy chains which raised and lowered the bridge, and, very slowly, the drawbridge began to rise.

"Look at the drawbridge!" squawked one of the goblins. "Go faster! We have to get out!"

The biggest goblin put his foot down and the van shot forwards.

"It's no good!" Rachel cried. "The drawbridge isn't lifting fast enough!"

A Piece
of Cake

As the van careered towards the rising drawbridge, Flora
flicked her wrist, sending more fairy magic streaming
through the air. Rachel and Kirsty held their breath. Just
as the goblins reached the drawbridge, it swung swiftly
upwards and slammed closed, trapping the goblins' van
inside the castle.

"Thanks, Flora," Kirsty said.

Flora winked at her, then waved her wand again and turned Rachel and Kirsty back to their human size. They all hurried over to the van.

"Now, give my cousin's cake back," Kirsty said firmly. "Or Flora will send you all to the castle dungeons!"

The goblin in the driver's seat looked sulky. He muttered something under his breath, and, the next moment, the back doors of the van

swung open. The goblins pushed the cake out onto the

flagstones. *Splat!*

Kirsty and Rachel looked at each other in dismay. The

tiers of the cake had collapsed, and the beautiful cake

was completely ruined!

"Well, at least the magic figurine isn't broken," Kirsty said, picking it up carefully. "But everything else is!"

"Now let us out of here!" the goblin driver yelled crossly. Flora waved her wand again, and, with a creak, the drawbridge slowly lowered. The goblins immediately sped away.

"Don't worry, girls, now I've got the figurine back, I can fix it," Flora said comfortingly. Then she grinned. "In fact, it will be a piece of cake!"

As she spoke, she sent a swirl of fairy magic in the direction of the ruined cake on the floor. The mess vanished in an instant, and, in the twinkling of an eye,

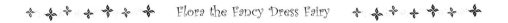

a beautiful, glittering five-tiered cake appeared, with little arches holding up each layer. White and pink iced flowers tumbled down the sides of the cake, and, as well as the magic figurine on top, small figures in fancy dress danced in between the different layers.

"Oh!" Kirsty breathed, "It's the most amazing cake I've
ever seen!"

Rachel nodded in agreement as a cardboard box
magically appeared and folded itself around the cake.
Just then, Lindsay and the delivery man came out into
the courtyard. Flora darted into Kirsty's pocket.

Looking excited, Lindsay opened the cake box. "Oh!"
she exclaimed in awe. "What a beautiful cake! It's
turned out even better than I imagined!"

"It is lovely, isn't it?" Rachel said with a grin.

"Magical!" Lindsay sighed, and the girls exchanged a secret smile.

"You know, I was worried because everything in the kitchens just now has been awful!" Lindsay went on.

"The chefs were getting all the recipes wrong, and the ovens weren't working properly. But this fabulous cake has made me feel a lot better!" She turned to the delivery man. "Could you help me carry it inside, please?"

"Everything will be fine in the kitchens now that the magic figurine is back, girls," Flora whispered, flying out of Kirsty's pocket.

"Thank goodness," Rachel said.

"I must return to Fairyland," Flora went on,

"but I'll be back — and so will Jack Frost's goblins, so be on your guard!" And, with that, she blew the girls a kiss and vanished.

Rachel and Kirsty smiled at each other, looking determined. They'd saved Flora's magic figurine and s the party food wouldn't be ruined, but what tricks would Jack Frost's goblins try next?

Colourful Costumes

"Jack Frost must be annoyed that his goblins didn't get away with the cake!" Rachel said to Kirsty with a smile. It was the following morning and the girls were walking downstairs into the entrance hall of the castle. Sunshine was streaming in through the arched windows, and everyone else was bustling here and there, busy with final preparations for the party that evening.

"Yes, so we must keep a look-out for more goblin mischief today," Kirsty replied, as Lindsay hurried by, carrying a vase of flowers. "We haven't got to get ready for the party for ages yet, so shall we ask Lindsay if there's anything we can do?"

"Good idea," Rachel agreed.

The two girls went over to Lindsay.

"Can we help?" asked Kirsty.

"Oh, thank you!" Lindsay said gratefully, placing the flowers on a table. "The costumes arrived an hour ago and they've been put in one of the bedrooms. Do you think you could check them and make sure that all the outfits have the right accessories with them?"

The girls nodded, so Lindsay led them quickly towards one of the bedrooms on the second floor.

"Most of the guests will be arriving in the next couple of hours," Lindsay explained. "So they'll be coming to choose their costumes then, but you two can have first pick." She stopped outside a heavy wooden door. "They're all in here."

"Hee hee hee!"

Kirsty jumped as she heard a nasty little muffled giggle coming from inside the room. Unfortunately, she knew exactly who giggled like that: goblins! She glanced at Rachel and Lindsay. Kirsty could tell from Rachel's face that she'd heard it too, but luckily Lindsay hadn't noticed so far.

"So," Rachel said quickly, stepping in front of Lindsay so that she didn't open the door, "you want us to check that all the costumes are displayed properly?"

"Yes," Lindsay replied. "And just
make sure that Robin Hood has
got his bow and arrows, that
kind of thing."

"We'll be fine, Lindsay,"
Kirsty told her. "You can
leave us to it. You must have
lots to do!"

"Oh, yes," Lindsay agreed. "I
must check on the decorations
in the ballroom. Thank you, girls." And
she hurried off.

"Watch out for goblins!" Kirsty told Rachel as she
opened the door.

Rachel groaned as the door swung inward to reveal
two giggling goblins pulling costumes off the racks!

The room was a complete mess.

One rack of costumes had been knocked over

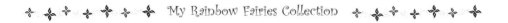

completely. And in the middle of the room there was a huge, messy heap of clothes. When the goblins saw the girls, they started grabbing armfuls of brightly-coloured costumes from the pile and throwing them out of the window.

"Stop that!" Rachel cried.

The goblins each seized another armful of clothes and then they both climbed onto the windowsill.

"They're going to jump!" Kirsty shouted.

As she and Rachel ran across the room, the goblins leapt out of the window, holding onto a thick, heavy rope. The girls saw that the rope had been tied to one of the wardrobes in the room. The other end dangled out of the window. The goblins were making their escape by lowering themselves down the castle wall, holding onto the rope.

"Look!" Kirsty cried, pointing down at the moat.

A rowing-boat was bobbing gently in the water. Three more goblins sat in the boat, surrounded by all the stolen costumes, hats and shoes that the two goblins had thrown out of the window.

Kirsty's heart sank as she spotted a bright red hooded cape on top of the pile. It was shimmering slightly with fairy magic.

"Oh, no!" she gasped. "They've got Flora's magic Red Riding Hood cape!"

Boat on the Moat

"Let's get down there!" Kirsty replied, running for the door with Rachel at her heels "What a shame Flora isn't here to turn us into fairies!"

The girls dashed down the stairs and into the entrance hall, which was now empty. Suddenly the visor in the suit of armour in the corner snapped open.

"Hello, girls!" called
a silvery voice, and Flora
zoomed out of the
visor. "Where are
you going in
such a hurry?"
"The goblins
have stolen
half the fancy
dress costumes,
including your
magic cape!"
Rachel explained.
"And they've got a boat
to escape across the moat!"
"We've got to stop them!" Flora exclaimed.
She and the girls raced out of the hall, through
the courtyard and onto the drawbridge.

"There they are!" Kirsty yelled, pointing.

The goblins were rowing furiously away from the

drawbridge towards the bend in the moat. As they

disappeared around the side of the castle, Rachel turned

to Flora. "We must stop them getting away!" she cried.

But Flora shook her head. "Don't worry, girls," she

replied calmly. "Just wait here."

Puzzled, Rachel and Kirsty glanced at each other. The goblins were escaping with the magic cape, and Flora didn't seem worried at all!

A moment later, Rachel and Kirsty heard the splashing of oars behind them. The girls spun round to see the silly goblins rowing towards them from around the other side of the castle.

"The goblins have gone round in a circle!" Kirsty laughed.

"They can't have realised that the moat surrounds the castle." Rachel and Flora grinned.

"Hey!" one of the goblins screeched suddenly. "There's the drawbridge. We're back where we started!"

"This is all your fault!" yelled another goblin, glaring at the two who were rowing the boat.

"I'm going to throw you into the moat, and the alligators will eat you!"

"I'm not scared of alligators!" shouted one of the

rowers. Then he paused. "Er, what's an alligator anyway?"

"I know what an alligator is," said one of the other goblins importantly. "It's pink and it has eight legs!"

"No, that's not an alligator," the first goblin yelled crossly. "That's an elephant!"

The goblins began to push and poke each other as they argued. The two who were rowing dropped their oars and joined in, and the boat began to drift aimlessly towards the drawbridge.

"Maybe we can lean over and grab the magic cape," Rachel whispered, as the boat approached.

"Especially as the goblins are arguing too much to take any notice of us," added Kirsty.

"Good idea." Flora nodded. "Let's go for it!"

Goblins Get Dressed

Rachel and Kirsty lay down on the drawbridge and dangled their arms over the moat as the boat drew nearer. But just as Rachel reached out her hand to snatch the sparkling red cape, one of the goblins looked up and spotted them.

"They're trying to steal our costumes!" he yelled, grabbing one of the oars. "Get away from the drawbridge! Row for the bank!"

Rachel, Kirsty and Flora watched in dismay as the goblins rowed away as fast as they could.

"I nearly got the cape, too," Rachel groaned, scrambling to her feet.

The goblins had reached the bank now and were throwing the costumes out of the boat onto the grass. Then they jumped out of the boat themselves. As Rachel, Kirsty and Flora rushed across the

drawbridge towards the boat, they heard the goblins yelling at each other. "There are too many costumes for us to carry!" one shouted. "What shall we do?"

"Put some of the clothes on!" screeched another goblin, struggling to get into a pair of red velvet breeches. He popped a white curly wig on his head, and then a sailor's hat on top. "We can carry the rest!"

As Flora and the girls hurried towards the bank, they watched in amazement as the goblins dressed themselves up. One put on a tiger outfit with a tail, and then a sparkly waistcoat, a clown's red nose, and three

hats, including a straw one with a plastic flower on it.
Another was wearing a pink clown wig with a golden
crown on top. He also had the magic cape slung round
his neck, but the hood kept falling forwards over his
face; because the costumes were human-sized, they were
much too big for the goblins. All of them were wearing
odd shoes which didn't fit, and they kept tripping over as
they rushed around scooping up the rest of the outfits.
Flora, Rachel and Kirsty couldn't help laughing as they
reached the bank.

"Hand over those costumes!" Flora called in her
silvery voice.

"No!" shouted the
goblin with the
cape. "Jack Frost's
holding his party
here tonight, so you
won't be
needing these!"

His friends cackled
gleefully. Then one
of them picked up a long
princess gown and threw it right over Rachel and
Kirsty's heads, trapping Flora, too, who was fluttering
alongside the girls.

"Help!" Rachel cried.

"Everything's gone dark!" Kirsty gasped.

Goblins
Meet Goats

As the girls and Flora struggled to free themselves from
the heavy dress, they heard the goblins rushing away,
chuckling.

"We have to catch them!" Rachel panted as she and
Kirsty finally managed to throw off the dress.

"Look, they've left some of the costumes behind," said Kirsty, pointing at a heap of clothes on the bank.

Rachel looked worried. "We can't leave them here in case Lindsay finds them," she said, picking up an embroidered jacket. "But we can't carry them while we run after the goblins either."

Kirsty frowned as she looked more closely at the jacket Rachel was holding. "The sleeves are almost falling off!" she exclaimed, pointing at the jacket.

"Look, the stitches are loose."

"That's because the magic cape is missing," Flora
explained. "The costumes are starting to fall apart at
the seams!"

"Oh, no!" Rachel sighed. "The party will be ruined if
we don't get the cape back."

Kirsty turned to Flora.

"Flora, could you shrink the costumes?" she
suggested eagerly. "Then they'd fit into
our pockets!"

"Sure!" Flora laughed,
waving her wand.

A swirl of fairy
dust later, and a
neat pile of tiny
clothes, shoes and
hats lay on the
bank. Rachel and

Kirsty knelt down and carefully filled their pockets. Then they raced off after the goblins.

The goblins had set off across the moors. Luckily Flora and the girls could see the magic cape shimmering

ahead of them in the distance, so they could easily keep track of where the goblins were going.

"Look, there's a cowboy hat," Rachel panted, seeing the hat lying on the grass.

"And there's a pink clown wig," Kirsty added, pointing a little further ahead. "The goblins must have dropped them."

Quickly, Flora shrunk the hat and the wig and the girls popped them into their pockets. Then they hurried after the goblins, picking up other fancy dress items that the goblins had dropped along the way.

A bit further on, Kirsty stopped and shaded her eyes, peering ahead to see where the goblins were. She saw them climbing a steep slope, heading up a mountain,

towards a herd of mountain goats. That gave Kirsty an idea. "Somehow we have to get the goblins to stop so that we can catch up!" Kirsty said urgently to Flora. "Do you think your magic could ask those goats to help us?"

"What a great idea!" Flora beamed. She pointed her wand at the goats and a stream of green and blue bubbles floated through the air towards the herd. The bubbles drifted towards the goats' ears and then burst gently, making little bleating sounds.

"Baa Baa!"

"That's goat language," Flora explained, as Rachel and Kirsty smiled.

The goats looked up from the grass. Then, as Flora and the girls watched, all the goats trotted over to stand in front of the goblins, blocking their path.

The goblins skidded to a halt and stared nervously at the hairy creatures. Flora, Rachel and Kirsty hurried to catch up. As they got closer, they could see the goblins shaking with fear.

"Are these alligators?" asked one fearfully.

"No," said the one with the cape. "I think they might be Pogwurzels!"

"Pogwurzels?" chorused the others in alarm.

"Yes. And we all know that Pogwurzels eat goblins!" the one with the cape wailed.

All the goblins shrieked with terror as one of the goats trotted forward. It leaned over to sniff the plastic flower on the straw hat.

"Please don't eat me, Mr Pogwurzel!" the goblin wearing the hat begged, too petrified to move.

"He looks hungry!" Rachel called, although she was secretly quite sure that goats didn't eat goblins.

"Maybe they want to eat the clothes," shouted Kirsty, as another goat sniffed at a goblin's sleeve.

Immediately, all the goblins threw down the clothes they were carrying. The goats sniffed curiously at the costumes but then turned their attention back to the goblins. With shrieks of fear, the goblins quickly pulled off all the items they were wearing.

The one with the magic cape took that off last of all. "Don't gobble me up, Mr Pogwurzel!" he begged, holding the cape out towards one of the goats. "This cloak is much tastier than I am."

The goat snorted, which was too much for the goblin. He squealed with fright, threw the cape on the ground and fled, his goblin friends charging after him.

Costume Clear-up

Flora, Rachel and Kirsty laughed.

"The goats won't really eat the costumes, will they?" Kirsty asked anxiously as the goats sniffed at the pile of costumes.

Flora shook her head as she shrank all the costumes, including the magic cape, so that the girls could gather them up and put them in their pockets. "Goats like

young thistle plants best of all," she said. And with
another wave of her wand, she turned a
large patch of purple heather

into a field of thistles. The
goats immediately bent
their heads, took a sniff
and began to gobble the
thistles up.

"Thank you, goats!"
called Flora and the girls
as they set off back to
McKersey Castle.

"Weren't the goblins silly?" Rachel laughed as they
hurried back across the drawbridge.

Kirsty nodded. "And they did look funny wearing all
those costumes," she added.

Soon they were back in the room where the fancy
dress costumes were stored. The girls looked dismayed as

they glanced around.

"I'd forgotten how much mess the goblins had made!" Kirsty sighed, staring at the overturned rack and the costumes strewn about. "How will we ever get this cleared up before Lindsay comes back?"

"No problem!" Flora announced cheerfully. "Leave this to me."

The little fairy danced around the room, flicking her wand here and there and sending little puffs of magical fairy dust whirling down onto the costumes. Rachel and Kirsty watched in delight as the clothes lifted themselves up off the floor and floated in the air. Then they danced over to the racks, sleeves waving. The hats and wigs

bobbed through the air
too, and all the shoes
began to tap dance
their way over to join
their costumes.

"Look!" Rachel said to
Kirsty. "All the clothes,
hats and shoes are sorting
themselves into the right outfits!"

Kirsty nodded as the curly pink wig
bobbed past to join the red nose, stripy trousers and
enormous shoes of the clown costume.

Then the tiny clothes began floating
out of the girls' pockets. As they
danced through the air, the
costumes grew back to
their normal sizes before
finding their places on

the racks. And Rachel noticed that, with the
magic cape safe and sound, the
sleeves on the embroidered
jacket weren't loose any more.

"This is brilliant, Flora!"
Kirsty exclaimed as the last
few pieces of the costumes
moved into place. "Look at
this, Rachel. All the men's
costumes are here, and the
ladies' costumes are on this
rack here."

"And the animal costumes
are on a separate rack,"
Rachel added, pointing at the tiger
costume and others. "Thank you so much, Flora. All the
costumes look perfect!"

Flora beamed at them. "You've got one item left in

your pocket, Kirsty," she said. And, as she spoke, the magic red cape floated out.

"I want someone special to wear it," Flora said thoughtfully. "Let me see… Aha!" Her face lit up and she lifted her wand. Immediately, the Red Riding Hood dress and basket lifted themselves off the rack and floated over to settle on a chair. The magic cape drifted over to join them, growing back to its normal size as it did so. Last of all, a big white label appeared in a burst of magic sparkles and pinned itself to the cape. "'Mrs Tate'," Kirsty read aloud. "Rachel, that costume's for my mum!"

With a gleam in her eyes, Flora tapped her wand on the chair. A furry grey wolf costume instantly appeared, with a label saying 'Mr Tate'. Kirsty and Rachel burst out laughing.

"That's fantastic, Flora!" Kirsty said gratefully. "Thank you."

"And thank you, girls," Flora said with a wide smile. "But don't forget that Jack Frost will still be doing his very best to stop the party from going ahead. Or, should I say, his very worst!"

Kirsty and Rachel nodded.

"We'll be careful," Rachel promised.

"Now I must go back to Fairyland, and you two had better choose yourself some fancy dress costumes," Flora said with a wink. "I'm sure that you'll find the costumes if you look hard enough!"

And as Rachel and Kirsty waved, the little fairy disappeared in a colourful swirl of glittering fairy magic.

Lindsay's Angels

"Hello, girls!" The door opened and Lindsay came in.
"Wow! You've done a great job!" she declared, looking
around.

Rachel and Kirsty smiled. Flora's magic had finished
tidying the room just in time.

"And have you chosen your outfits?" Lindsay asked.
Rachel and Kirsty glanced at each other excitedly. Flora
had said that she was sure they'd find the perfect fancy
dress costumes. Had she worked some fairy magic and
left special outfits just for them?

Kirsty's face lit up as she suddenly noticed a few blue
and green sparkles floating around one of the racks.

"Actually, we were just about to have a look," she said, nudging Rachel.

Rachel spotted the sparkles too, and together the two girls hurried over to the rack. There, hanging at one end, they found two beautiful angel costumes. The dainty white dresses sparkled with a silver sheen and there were matching feathery wings, delicate haloes and silver cardboard angel harps. White feather masks glittering with silver sparkles completed the outfits.

Rachel and Kirsty looked at each other in delight as
they took the gorgeous costumes off the rack.

"We'd love to wear
these outfits," Kirsty said
to Lindsay.

"Well, I don't even
remember seeing
those," Lindsay said
with a smile, "but
they are lovely and

they'll suit you both perfectly!"

They all turned round as the door opened again and
Mr and Mrs Tate came in, followed by several couples.

"All the guests have arrived now, so we're bringing
them to choose their costumes," Mrs Tate explained.
Lindsay smiled at everyone. "Why don't you go and
change?" she said to the girls. "Then go and have a peep
at the ballroom decorations."

Rachel and Kirsty nodded happily.

"Mum, Dad," Kirsty called as she headed for the door
with her angel outfit. "Your costumes are on the chair."
Mr and Mrs Tate laughed in delight when they saw the
Red Riding Hood and wolf costumes. Laughing too,
Rachel and Kirsty hurried off to their room.

"I'll help you put up your hair, and then you can help
me with mine," Rachel said as they slipped the pretty
white dresses on. "Then we can fix the haloes on top."

Soon the girls were ready.

"Don't our costumes look fantastic?" Rachel said as
they stood side by side admiring themselves in
the mirror.

"Yes, thanks to Flora," Kirsty agreed happily.

"Let's go downstairs and look at the ballroom," suggested Rachel.

"The party will be starting soon, and I can't wait!" Carrying their harps, the girls went downstairs to the enormous ballroom. The doors stood open and Rachel and Kirsty peeped inside. The room was empty as all the other guests were still dressing.

"Isn't it beautiful?" Kirsty breathed.

The ballroom was decorated in white and gold. There were long white curtains, held back by twisted golden ropes at the windows, glittering crystal chandeliers hanging from the ceiling, and sprays of white roses on all the tables. There were also white marble statues wearing beautiful fancy dress masks placed around the room.

"I don't think any of these masks are Flora's magic one," remarked Rachel. "Don't forget that we have to make sure the goblins don't get hold of it, Kirsty, or the party will be ruined!"

Kirsty nodded. "There's the cake," she said, pointing to a table at the other end of the room. The girls went to have a closer look and placed their harps on the table. "It looks even more beautiful here in the ballroom," Rachel said admiringly.

But Kirsty was distracted by a blue and emerald figurine on the cake's middle tier. "Look!" she exclaimed. "That figure looks just like Flora!"

"Yes, it does," Rachel agreed. Suddenly the figurine winked at them! Rachel and Kirsty were so startled, they almost dropped their harps.

"It's Flora!" Kirsty laughed.

"Hello," called Flora, zipping over to the girls with a big smile.

Before Rachel could reply, a movement out in the courtyard caught her eye. She glanced out of the window and saw a group of rather odd-looking guests. They were very short and had extremely large feet.

"Goblins!" Rachel gasped in dismay. "They're arriving for Jack Frost's party!"

Goblin
Guests

"We must stop them!" Flora said firmly, and the three friends rushed out of the ballroom.

There were five goblins outside, all dressed in top hats and tails. They were heading towards the entrance hall door as Flora, Rachel and Kirsty emerged into the courtyard.

"Hello!" Rachel called quickly, "Are you coming to Lindsay and Robert's party?"

"No!" snapped one of the goblins. "We're going to Jack
Frost's party!"

"Oh, that's not here," Kirsty put in. "I expect it will be at
his ice castle."

Muttering grumpily, the goblin
pulled out a large invitation
card. "It says here that Jack
Frost's party is taking
place at McKersey
Castle!" he said loudly.
The girls glanced nervously
at Flora. The little fairy
grinned and aimed her wand
at the invitation. A few magic
sparkles went zooming towards it.

"Tell him to check again!" she whispered to Kirsty.

"Are you sure you haven't made a mistake?" Kirsty
asked the goblin.

"Of course!" the goblin said rudely, shoving the invitation under the girls' noses. "It says—" But then he stopped, his eyes almost popping out of his head as they all read the swirly, silver writing: 'Jack Frost's ice castle'.

"The party is at Jack Frost's ice castle!" the goblin mumbled sheepishly.

The other goblins looked confused. Muttering angrily, they all turned round and slunk away.

"And tell your friends," Kirsty called after them, "that Jack Frost won't be happy if his guests are late!"

"Good!" Flora said with satisfaction,
hiding on Kirsty's shoulder as
the girls went inside. "That
will keep some of the goblin
guests away."

Inside the entrance hall
people were gathering for the
start of the party. Rachel and
Kirsty smiled to see a man
dressed as a scarecrow. He was
standing rigidly in the corner
with his arms stuck out.

"He's acting just like a real scarecrow!" Rachel
whispered to Kirsty. "Isn't that funny?"

Kirsty nodded as a man in a cowboy outfit strolled
towards them. "Howdy, girls," he said in an American
accent, tipping his hat.

Rachel and Kirsty couldn't help laughing.

"Grrr!"

Startled by the sound of
growling, the girls looked
round. A woman dressed
in the tiger outfit was
staring at them. Then
she sprang forward and
Rachel and Kirsty had to
jump out of the way.

"She's taking her costume
a bit seriously!" Rachel whispered as the tiger
woman began sharpening her claws.

Just then Lindsay rushed into the entrance hall. She
wasn't wearing her costume and she looked very upset.

"What's the matter, Lindsay?" asked Kirsty anxiously.

"My mask is missing!" Lindsay said, "and I don't know
where it's gone. It's a complete mystery! It's black with
rainbow-coloured feathers. Have you seen it?"

Rachel and Kirsty shook their heads, glancing at each other in dismay.

They recognised the description: it was the magic mask!

"The goblins must have stolen my mask," Flora whispered, as Lindsay hurried round the entrance hall, asking the other guests.

"Is that why the guests are behaving so strangely?" Kirsty asked.

Flora nodded. "Yes," she said anxiously. "The fairy magic in your lockets must be protecting you two, but I think the other guests are becoming their fancy dress characters!"

Missing Mask

"Oh, no!" Rachel whispered. "Remember all those crazy costumes we sorted out? We have to find the magic mask or this party will be chaos!"

"Lindsay, we'll help you look," Kirsty called to her cousin. "Where did you last have your mask?"

Lindsay frowned. "I had it in the ballroom," she said slowly, "and I had it in the wine cellar when I went to get a bottle of champagne."

"We'll look in the cellar while you search the

ballroom," Rachel suggested.

Lindsay nodded. "Thanks, girls."

The entrance to the wine

cellar wasn't far from the

entrance hall. Rachel

and Kirsty climbed down

the staircase into the stone

cellar and began to look

around.

"What's that?" Kirsty asked,

pointing at the flagstones.

There was a fine layer of dust on the floor and the

girls and Flora could see

footprints. Next to

them lay a tiny

pink feather.

"That's a feather

from the magic mask!" Flora exclaimed. "And those are goblin footprints. Let's follow them."

The footprints led to a wall at the back of the cellar, where they stopped abruptly.

"Did the goblins use Jack Frost's magic to walk through the wall?" Kirsty wondered.

The girls peered closely at the wall and moved their hands over it carefully.

"I can feel a draught of air here!" Rachel said excitedly, with her hand on the join between two stones.

"A secret door!" Flora exclaimed.

Just then Rachel noticed a smooth, round indentation in one of the stones. She pressed it and immediately the wall swung back slowly. Rachel, Kirsty and Flora stared at the dark passageway that stretched away behind the wall.

"The goblins must have escaped down this secret passage with the mask," Kirsty said.

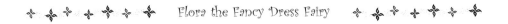

"Yes, I wonder where it goes," Rachel replied. "It's too dark to see." She looked nervous. "Jack Frost and his goblins might be hiding in there!"

Immediately Flora swished her wand lightly back and forth, and the tip began to glow with a bright light. Now Rachel and Kirsty could see into the passage ahead.

The three friends crept down the narrow corridor until they found themselves face to face with another stone wall.

"Oh!" Rachel said, disappointedly. "It's a dead end."

"Maybe not," Kirsty replied. She ran her hands over the stones and found a round indentation the same as the one that had opened the other wall. Kirsty pressed it and the wall began to move.

"Don't open it all the way, Kirsty," Flora hissed. "We don't know what's on the other side!"

Quickly, Kirsty took her finger off the indentation, so that the wall stayed open just a crack.

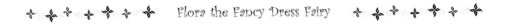

The girls and Flora peered through the narrow opening. Behind it was not a passageway, but they could see a cave-like room instead. They could also hear a familiar voice…

"Now, listen to me, goblins!" it was saying. "I'm going to tell you exactly how to ruin this pesky party!"

"Oh, no!" Kirsty whispered. "It's Jack Frost!"

Jack Frost Unmasked!

"I want you to steal every mask in the castle!" Jack Frost declared gleefully, sitting in a big chair before his goblins, his back to the girls. "And you must cause as much trouble as you can, while you're doing it. We have to get rid of these annoying humans!"

"Look at the mask in Jack Frost's hand," Rachel whispered.

Kirsty and Flora stared at the mask. It was black with rainbow-coloured, plumy feathers, and it shimmered slightly with magic.

"It's my magic mask," Flora said softly.

"I'm going to wear this mask because it's the best one, and I'm the most important person!" Jack Frost said boastfully, waving it in the air.

"He doesn't realise it's the magic mask," Flora said to Rachel and Kirsty.

"But how are we going to get it away from him?" Rachel asked.

"He's very close," Kirsty pointed out. "Maybe I can just grab the mask and we can make a run for it?"

"Let's try it," Flora agreed. "Once we have the mask, I'll use

my magic to block the
entrance to the secret
passage so that you
can escape."

Kirsty nodded,
feeling extremely
nervous as she edged
her way carefully through
the gap. She hoped that the goblins wouldn't spot her.
Luckily, she was hidden by Jack Frost's chair.

"Now go and make sure every human in this castle
is gone as soon as possible!" Jack Frost shouted at his
goblins, waving the mask about again.

At that moment, Kirsty leaned forward and snatched
the mask right out of Jack Frost's hand.

Jack Frost whipped round. "Stop that girl!" he roared,
and all the goblins surged forward as Kirsty darted back
into the passageway.

Rachel pulled the door closed behind Kirsty just as Jack Frost lifted his wand.

"This will stop them," said Flora, and she sent a whoosh of magical fairy dust towards the wall. The sparkles framed the door with a glittering outline, sealing it firmly shut.

Then Rachel, Kirsty and Flora dashed off down the secret passage.

A few moments later they were back in the entrance hall.

"That was close!" Rachel exclaimed. "I'm sure Jack Frost was about to cast a horrible spell!"

"You did brilliantly, Kirsty," Flora put in. "Now let's get the magic mask back to Lindsay as quickly as we can."

"There are Lindsay and Robert," Kirsty murmured. "Don't they look great?"

Rachel nodded. "They look like the King and Queen of the Ball," she said with a smile.

Lindsay was dressed in a beautiful Tudor ballgown, with hooped skirts sewn with beads and sparkling jewels. Robert was wearing an embroidered jacket, knee breeches, and a stiff white ruff around his neck. They both wore gold crowns.

"Lindsay!" Kirsty called. "We found your mask."

Lindsay stared down her nose at the girls. "How dare you approach me in such a rude manner?" she snapped haughtily. "Be gone, immediately!"

Rachel and Kirsty stared at each other in confusion.

"It's OK," Flora whispered from Kirsty's shoulder. "Lindsay's just acting like a real queen because the mask isn't back in its proper place yet."

Quickly, Kirsty pressed the magic mask into Lindsay's hand. Immediately, Lindsay blinked a couple of times and then seemed to wake up, almost as though she'd been in a trance. Robert and all the other guests did the same.

"Thank you, girls," Lindsay said gratefully, as Rachel and Kirsty glanced at each other in relief.

"Now we can start the party!" Kirsty said with a smile.

Fancy Dress in Fairyland

Lindsay and Robert led the guests to the ballroom, but Rachel and Kirsty hung back until the entrance hall was empty.

"Jack Frost and his goblins will leave now that the magic mask is back in its rightful place," Flora told the girls. "It will make sure the party goes smoothly. So you will have nothing more to worry about."

"Thank you, Flora," Kirsty said gratefully. "Lindsay and Robert's party will be great now, thanks to you!"

"We did it together, girls!" Flora declared happily. Suddenly, there was a flash of coloured light and a

magical rainbow streamed into the entrance hall. Rachel and Kirsty grinned as Bertram, the frog footman, hopped off the end of it.

"Good evening!" Bertram said, bowing low. "The King and Queen of Fairyland would like to invite Kirsty and Rachel to drop in on their fancy dress party in the Grand Ballroom."

"Oh, yes, please!" the girls said eagerly.

Bertram ushered the girls onto the end of the rainbow and Flora flew to join them. Then they were whisked off to Fairyland in a whirl of rainbow colours.

When they arrived at the Fairyland palace, Kirsty and Rachel were thrilled to see everyone waiting for them. The Grand Ballroom had been decorated with glittering white and pink decorations, and all the fairies were in wonderful costumes.

"Welcome!" said King Oberon. He was dressed as
King Arthur, and Queen Titania was by his side, dressed
as Lady Guinevere.

"We want to thank you for making sure all Flora's
magic items are where they belong," the Queen told
them. "That means this party will be a success as well as
Lindsay's. And Jack Frost and his goblins are coming, too.
We sent them an invitation they couldn't refuse!"

Before Rachel and Kirsty could reply, a magic
rainbow streamed in through an open window,
depositing a scowling Jack Frost on the floor.

A moment later, another rainbow whooshed through

the same window, and all the goblins tumbled off
the end of it as if they were falling out of a chute.
Grumbling, they picked themselves up.

"You must be in costume to attend our party, Jack
Frost," King Oberon said firmly. "Flora's magic will
give you any fancy dress outfit you like. Now, what
will it be?"

Rachel and Kirsty watched as Jack Frost frowned
in thought.

"I want to be a pirate king!" he declared at last.

Flora fluttered over to him and
waved her wand over his head.
Sparkling fairy dust instantly
transformed Jack Frost into a pirate
king, complete with an eye-patch,
gold hoop earring and big black
boots. He was also wearing an
extremely large pirate hat.

Rachel and Kirsty grinned to see that the goblins were now wearing pirate costumes too. Some of them even had peg legs, and parrots on their shoulders.

Looking very pleased with himself, Jack Frost strode off towards the tables laden with party food. "Come along, me hearties!" he shouted in a piratical way.

"Aye-aye, Captain!" the goblins yelled. And they followed Jack Frost, waving their cutlasses enthusiastically.

"Don't worry," Flora told the girls, "the swords aren't sharp at all." She looked down at her mermaid costume. "It's a new party, so I need a new outfit!" she remarked.

Rachel and Kirsty watched as Flora waved her wand above her head. Purple and black sparkles surrounded her for a moment, and her mermaid tail changed to a black frilly dress.

A large black pointed hat appeared on her head, and suddenly she was hovering in the air on a broomstick.

"You're a witch!" Kirsty cried.

"A very friendly-looking witch," Rachel pointed out. And then she and Kirsty laughed as a tiny black cat appeared at the end of the broomstick, mewing loudly.

Flora grinned at them and flew down from her broomstick. The broom and the cat immediately followed her.

"Girls, thank you for coming," said Queen Titania, "but it's time for you to return to McKersey Castle."

Rachel and Kirsty gave Flora a big hug. Then all the fairies gathered round in their wonderful costumes to wave to the girls as the Queen raised her wand.

"Goodbye!" called Rachel and Kirsty as they were whisked away on a cloud of fairy magic.

Almost instantly, Rachel and Kirsty found themselves outside the ballroom at McKersey Castle. They could hear music playing inside, and people talking and laughing.

"It sounds like the party's going well," Rachel remarked, pushing open the doors as the girls walked through. But Kirsty wasn't listening. She was staring down at the harps on the table. "Rachel," she said softly,

in a thrilled voice, "our harps aren't cardboard any more.
The fairies must have made them real!"

She ran her fingers over the silver strings and four
clear, melodic notes rang out.

Rachel smiled dreamily at her own harp. "Isn't fairy magic wonderful?" she said, peeping into the ballroom where people were dancing beneath the glittering chandeliers. "Fairy magic is the best!" Kirsty agreed happily, and the girls went into the ballroom to join the party.

Have you read them all?

Also available as an ebook

The Rainbow Fairies

Ruby the Red Fairy • Amber the Orange Fairy • Saffron the Yellow Fairy

Fern the Green Fairy • Sky the Blue Fairy • Izzy the Indigo Fairy • Heather the Violet Fairy

The Weather Fairies

Crystal the Snow Fairy • Abigail the Breeze Fairy • Pearl the Cloud Fairy

Goldie the Sunshine Fairy • Evie the Mist Fairy • Storm the Lightning Fairy • Hayley the Rain Fairy

The Party Fairies

Cherry the Cake Fairy • Melodie the Magic Fairy • Grace the Glitter Fairy

Honey the Sweet Fairy • Polly the Party Fun Fairy • Phoebe the Fashion Fairy • Jasmine the Present Fairy

The Jewel Fairies

India the Moonstone Fairy • Scarlett the Garnet Fairy • Emily the Emerald Fairy

Chloe the Topaz Fairy • Amy the Amethyst Fairy • Sophie the Sapphire Fairy • Lucy the Diamond Fairy

The Pet Keeper Fairies

Katie the Kitten Fairy • Bella the Bunny Fairy • Georgia the Guinea Pig Fairy

Lauren the Puppy Fairy • Harriet the Hamster Fairy • Molly the Goldfish Fairy

The Fun Day Fairies

Megan the Monday Fairy • Tallulah the Tuesday Fairy • Willow the Wednesday Fairy

Thea the Thursday Fairy • Freya the Friday Fairy • Sienna the Saturday Fairy • Sarah the Sunday Fairy

The Petal Fairies

Tia the Tulip Fairy   Pippa the Poppy Fairy   Louise the Lily Fairy

Charlotte the Sunflower Fairy   Danielle the Daisy Fairy   Olivia the Orchid Fairy   Ella the Rose Fairy

The Dance Fairies

Bethany the Ballet Fairy   Rebecca the Rock 'n' Roll Fairy

Tasha the Tap Dance Fairy   Jessica the Jazz Fairy   Saskia the Salsa Fairy   Imogen the Ice Dance Fairy

The Sporty Fairies

Francesca the Football Fairy   Zoe the Skating Fairy

Naomi the Netball Fairy   Samantha the Swimming Fairy   Alice the Tennis Fairy   Gemma the Gymnastics Fairy

The Music Fairies

Poppy   Ellie the Guitar Fairy   Fiona the Flute Fairy

Danni the Drum Fairy   Maya the Harp Fairy   Victoria the Violin Fairy   Sadie

The Magical Animal Fairies

Ashley the Dragon Fairy   Lara the Black Cat Fairy   Erin the Firebird Fairy

Rihanna the Seahorse Fairy   Sophia the Snow Swan Fairy   Leona the Unicorn Fairy   Caitlin the Ice Bear Fairy

The Green Fairies

Nicole the Beach Fairy   Isabella the Air Fairy   Edie the Garden Fairy

Coral the Reef Fairy   Lily the Rainforest Fairy   Milly the River Fairy   Carrie the Snow Cap Fairy

The Ocean Fairies

The Twilight Fairies

The Showtime Fairies

The Princess Fairies

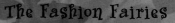

The Pop Star Fairies

The Fashion Fairies

The Sweet Fairies

The Baby Animal Rescue Fairies

The Holiday Specials

There's a book of fairy fun for everyone!

www.rainbowmagicbooks.co.uk

Fairy Farewell

We hope you've enjoyed reading our
adventures and that Jack Frost didn't
cause too much mischief!

Thank you being such a good fairy friend.
To reward you, we've created a special
friendship spell just for you
to share with your best friend:

Always caring, always sharing
Love and laughter with each other!
Friends together, friends forever!

Keep believing in fairy magic!

Fern
x

Flora
x

Ruby
x

Saffron
x

Sky
x

Amber
x

Izzy
x

Heather
x